DPS GREATER FARIDABAD
PRESENTS

YARN
WEAVING WORDS

Stories & Illustrations by Students of DPS Greater Faridabad

Editors
Suverchala Kashyap
Sumedha Kapur & Shweta Sehgal

Cover Page by Yajat Kapur

Ukiyoto Publishing

All global publishing rights are held by

Ukiyoto Publishing

Published in 2023

Content Copyright © DPS Greater Faridabad ISBN 9789360165598

All rights reserved.
No part of this publication may be reproduced, transmitted, or stored in a retrieval system, in any form by any means, electronic, mechanical, photocopying, recording or otherwise, without the prior permission of the publisher.

The moral rights of the author have been asserted. This is a work of fiction. Names, characters, businesses, places, events, locales, and incidents are either the products of the author's imagination or used in a fictitious manner. Any resemblance to actual persons, living or dead, or actual events is purely coincidental.

This book is sold subject to the condition that it shall not by way of trade or otherwise, be lent, resold, hired out or otherwise circulated, without the publisher's prior consent, in any form of binding or cover other than that in which it is published.

www.ukiyoto.com

*Celebrating a Decade
of Excellence
at
DPS Greater
Faridabad*

PREFACE

Books are magical, they open up innumerable worlds and immerse the reader in moments of fantasy, mystery and suspense. When we hold a book in our hand, it transports us into the author's mind and his or her reflections. It teleports one into realms that the author has envisaged and created. They are worlds that instantly take one on a spin. A book is not just about the content we read, it's a lot more than carefully chosen words strung together. It is a picture painted in words.

Even though it is said that a book should not be judged by its cover, the first thing that one is attracted by on entering a bookstore or a library, is the look of the book and the title, the feel of the paper as one gingerly flips through the alluring pages, the font, the illustrations and finally the creativity of the writer. In short, a book is a wholesome experience that awakens our senses, passion and imagination.

The thought of providing a platform for our students to showcase their creative talent on paper started taking shape and culminated as a concept into – YARN. We all loved the name and also came up with the full form – Young Authors and Readers Network. What started as a casual discussion, became an initiative.

The book *Yarn-Weaving Words*, is not just about stories, it's the process that each one of us associated with it, has experienced. We decided to make our book a complete learning experience, so we collaborated with students who wanted to write stories and those who wanted to illustrate them; most of them, who had never had such an experience before. Peer discussions, mentors' feedback and reviews of stories helped them understand each other's point of view better.

Team work was exemplary, enthused and exhilarating with our talented alumni students pitching in with equal zeal and maneuvering through the process for cover page design and other details. The mission was accomplished with ease. Ideating, editing, formatting and weaving the words into a book, fuelled our creative prowess & ended up being an extremely gratifying experience. The enthusiasm of all the students was immeasurable and their dedication to complete their tasks even during their final or board exams is the spirit of this book – *It's not life that matters but the courage we bring to it!*

All the stories and illustrations are woven into this theme and present a kaleidoscope of thoughts of our young Dipsites, their characters coming alive though their plots, enduring the challenges of life and overcoming them with grace and courage. Each story takes us into a different dimension of life, a soul-searching journey, yet, embedded & etched into one consciousness it unleashes the latent fount of courage in all of us.

ACKNOWLEDGEMENT

Highlighting the joy of creative collaboration – "YARN' has emerged as a beautiful tapestry fabricated over time where vibrant hues, vivid imaginations and emotions that accompany a writer's journey create a unique design. We invoke the blessings of God Almighty by expressing our gratitude to HIM for guiding us from the very inception to the completion of this project.

"Trust gives you the permission to give people direction, get everyone aligned and gives them energy to go get the job done. It enables you to execute with excellence and produce extraordinary results."

We dedicate this work to our dear Principal Ma'am, Mrs. Surjeet Khanna for being the wind beneath our wings. We thank her for believing in each one of us, for inspiring and motivating us at all times, to capture the essence, talent and spirit of DIPSITES. We would also like to thank our Pro VC Mr. Rohit Jainendra Jain for his guidance and support.

Team YARN will always be indebted to our mentor Mrs. Suverchala Kashyap for her incessant support through her mentoring sessions and constant guidance. Without her valuable inputs and suggestions, this Herculean task would not have been possible. We would also like to thank Mrs. Manjit Legha for her insight and guidance.

Illustrations help readers visualize characters, setting and mood of the story and our team of student illustrators from DPSGF played with their creativity to bring the stories to life. We are immensely thankful to our alumni mentors Mr. Abhinav Kumar, Mr. Steve Adolphus for their selfless investment in mentoring our team of illustrators and Mr. Yajat Kapur for designing the book cover.

Last but not the least, we extend our gratitude to each and every person who helped bring this book to fruition.

FOREWORD

Courage is jostling with the turmoil within and around us, emerging triumphant and being a better version of ourselves in the pursuit of comprehending the world. It is to tread on untrodden paths, to carve the curve of your life with its share of vicissitudes.

YARN is the affirmation of the courage that manifests in our hearts which gives us the encouragement to harness our creative pursuits. The young minds, abound with vivid imagination and innovative ideas possess a fascinating zeal to reach out to the world. The initiative YARN – Young Authors and Readers Network provides venues for our aspiring Dipsites to express their creative imagination through their stories and illustrations.

The theme of the book – 'It's not life that matters but the courage we bring to it!' resonates with the aspirations of Yarn and this book 'Weaving Words' is a testimony to it. With the iridescent display of imagination, each story, written and illustrated by the teenage authors and illustrators of DPS Greater Faridabad, reflects a mature voice.

The fear deeply inset in the recesses of the mind, the courage to endure it, or conquer it, validating the efforts in adversity, fulfilling one's purpose in life, struggle to achieve dreams, relatable characters and the illustrations exquisitely emoting the essence of every story make these stories come alive in the readers' mind. The cover page designed by our alumni, Yajat Kapur, highlights attention to detail and adds to the aesthetic flavour.

Every story takes us into a different realm and yet they all are so beautifully strewn together in congruence with the theme, words woven into a pattern of beautiful thoughts.

I congratulate the Yarn team of mentors, Mrs. Suverchala Kashyap, Mrs. Sumedha

Kapur and Mrs. Shweta Sehgal as well my students for the first edition of the book 'Yarn – Weaving Words'. I am sure this book will stir the emotions and find a place in every reader's heart.

Mrs. Surjeet Khanna
Principal
DPS Greater Faridabad

MENTOR'S TAKE

Ms. Suverchala Kashyap
Founder Director Parivartan
SK's Transformational Hub

In the poem 'All things bright and beautiful,' Cecil F. Alexander, describes the bounty of nature and the things that tug at our heartstrings...the words that impacted me are:

The purple-headed mountain,
the river running by,
The sunset, and the morning,
that brightens up the sky;

All of us are enamoured by different things and anything to do with words brings a smile to my face. Thus, the idea of putting together a book of short stories by children, was not only extremely fascinating but one that resonated with me: providing a platform where everyone gets a chance to put forth their views and create a tapestry that is imbued with different hues. The over-arching theme is very close to my heart too and the children have tried to portray their inherent creativity by moulding it to their understanding, thereby creating a magic of sorts. I am certain that all age groups will revel in the depth of their knowledge and creativity.

Ms. Shweta Sehgal
Educator, DPS Greater Faridabad

Having an idea to write a book can be easy, beginning to write may also seem easy, but writing a book to the finish is an adventurous journey. Taking random threads and weaving them into a tapestry of words and illustrations through YARN, was one such journey en route which I discovered many different perspectives through different characters of the stories. It was also a realisation of striving to traverse the path less followed and foraging a new path for ourselves.

Ms. Sumedha Kapur
Educator, DPS Greater Faridabad

Yarn is the versatile thread that can be woven into myriad possibilities, just as thoughts, when woven into words have the ability to create powerful tales. YARN has given me an opportunity to get an insight into the young minds, look at the world with a fresh perspective through their stories and illustrations; it has helped me understand that 'Courage' can be manifested in different forms in our lives, be it in endurance, in trust, in acceptance or in overcoming our challenges.

Index
Authors of Our Tales

- ❖ **The Sonder of Our Heartstrings**   2
  - Pratishtha Mohanty

- ❖ **Antale**   17
  - Jayati Kapur

- ❖ **The Red Bag**   39
  - Pakhi Arora

- ❖ **Fortitude**   53
  - Nysa Mishra

- ❖ **The Courage She Had**   67
  - Lavanya Mittal

- ❖ **Jewels in the Eyes**   79
  - Attrija Abhijit Gitay

- ❖ **Life -A Hill of Ups and Downs**   97
  - Pakhi Gupta

- ❖ **The Ghostly Nightmares**   115
  - Preeyam Das

- ❖ **All it takes is a Drop of Courage**   133
  - Arnav Bhattacharya

- ❖ **The Nostalgic Smile**   **145**
  - Prisha Koshal

- ❖ **The Power of Destiny**   **157**
  - Garima Singh Chauhan

- ❖ **Fight for Justice**   **175**
  - Kriti Bansal

- ❖ **Staring Into the Night Sky**   **187**
  - Anubhav Dash

- ❖ **Dared to Dream**   **205**
  - Anusha Sharma

- ❖ **Can we Meet**   **219**
  - Parnika Pande

Illustrators of Our Tales

- **The Sonder of Our Heartstrings**
  Pratishtha Mohanty
- **Antale**   Mudit Jha
- **The Red Bag**   Rishit Mittal
- **Fortitude**   Rishit Mittal
- **The Courage She Had**   Sehar Yadav
- **Jewels in the Eyes**   Saara Gaur
- **Life -A Hill of Ups and Downs**
  Rishit Mittal
- **The Ghostly Nightmares**
  Arpita Patel
- **All it Takes is a Drop of Courage**
  Devarsh Bhatia
- **The Nostalgic Smile**   Devarsh Bhatia
- **The Power of Destiny**   Arpita Patel
- **Fight For Justice**   Sehar Yadav
- **Staring Into the Night Sky**
  Yashvardhan Singh
- **Dared to Dream**   Devarsh Bhatia
- **Can we Meet**   Pratishtha Mohanty

It is Not Life that

Matters

but the Courage

You bring to it!

Author & Illustrator: The Sonder of Our Heartstrings

Pratishtha Mohanty

Pratishtha is seventeen-year-old. She has always loved to read, enjoys interacting with others to improve her writing, and is an intellectual who relishes learning something new every day.

DPS GREATER FARIDABAD

The Sonder of Our Heartstrings
By Pratishtha Mohanty

"The trash is supposed to be recycled, Josh!" Meredith yells.

"The lunch has to be set on the table too! What are you busy doing?" James screeched in that deep heavy, groggy voice of his while looking for me.

Josh, I'm Josh. Despite being young and full of life, 21-year-old me is trapped taking care of his elderly grandparents ever since my parents died in a horrific car accident.

Feeling obliged, cornered, and responsible for the old couple, I can't help but swallow the inner frustration I feel for not being able to live like an average person of my age.

'Was it a good thing to be different like this or should I despise it?' These questions may remain unanswered for a long time.
As if sacrificing my youth wasn't enough, I not only have to earn for myself but for two

YARN – WEAVING WORDS

other people enclosed in this small, humble abode of ours. My grandfather's monthly pensions are sufficient to meet my daily needs, but in order to meet my pleasures and desires, I must consign myself to working like an ox.

My childhood was passing by so quickly, my grandparents were getting older every day, finances were getting tight, and the thing that hurt the most was that I had no one to lean on, no one to talk to about my feelings—just me and my chamber in the attic.

Furthermore, life on the outskirts of London wasn't as picturesque as it seemed. Being surrounded by nature may occasionally become overpowering. Having nowhere to go except outside with nothing but vast expanses of green, verdant patches of grass all around you can both provide serenity and, at the same time, cause you to be overpowered by loneliness. Contrarily, everyone is familiar with the term 'seasickness,' but I'm not sure if anyone would comprehend the enormity of 'land sickness' that I experienced.

The couple was residing in the other two rooms after being compelled to move into the old, dusty attic that was nearly ready to collapse at any moment.

James grunts when I make him sit at our dining table, surrounded by three ramshackle chairs barely able to keep up with our weight anymore. Gently lifting him and settling his legs on the footrest in front, I resume placing the lunch for both of them while pushing my hunger aside.

'Priorities Josh. Remember the priorities.'
I mumble to myself while carrying out the designated chores.

Before I could proceed to have a seat on the countertop of our mini-kitchen to catch a breath and relax, my trail of thoughts was interrupted by Meredith yelling from the other room. Did I fail to mention before that this couple is far from being a couple?

YARN – WEAVING WORDS

Getting along does not exist in their dictionary.

Before I could even comprehend the situation, my mind couldn't help but go into a flashback, the flashback of us, just me and my grandparents when we all were healthy and most of all happy. I don't deny the fact that we still are happy, but the kind of happiness that cannot even be registered by the person themselves be even valid enough to be labeled as happiness ?

Meredith was dying with laughter as she tried to act irate on us for delaying our having dinner together while we were playing outside in the rain with my James jumping around in the dirty pools along with me.

Meredith's shrill voice again stopped me before I could proceed down the path of nostalgia.

"Will you stop putting all your attention on the poor old creature and help me out here?! I need to change for my afternoon nap right here, Josh!"

The irony of life can be truly astounding at times. how once her soft voice would call out to James with a nickname coated in pure honey and now he is just thrashed around as a poor old creature.

As soon as her words reached my ears, I knew what was coming my way. Before contemplating the harshness of her words in more depth, I made my way towards her room. The soft sounds made by my slippers when I would drag my feet along the wooden floor would only make me feel as if this was the silence before the storm.

Meredith has been diagnosed with IED or Intermittent Explosive Disorder. Impulsive episodes of anger, violence, and ruthlessness here and there were common for me.

As if all of this wasn't enough, James... wasn't mentally stable either. He is diagnosed with 'Peter Pan syndrome,' which we call 'the little space.' His body is growing old with age, but his mind still functions like the child he once was whenever he is triggered.

Taking care of both of them is like taking care of an old lady transitioning to her menopause stage 24/7 and a five year-old pampered child breathing down her neck.

"I. Told. You. I. Wanted. Red. Bedsheets laid out on my bed for today! I mentioned it to you seven times yesterday, but your peanut-sized brain failed to process my words!"

Hag is an evil old woman not man so replaced it with creature.

Meredith's words brought me back to reality. Being used to the harshness, I just closed my eyes, took a deep breath, 'inhale…exhale…Josh' and opening my eyes, I made eye contact with her and said, "It seems you're really hurt, Meredith."
Rule number one: Make sure not to let out your own frustration on the subject, make them realize that you know they're hurt.

Meredith's face contorted into a frown, her eyebrows furrowing, her breathing fastening, and her eyelids pooling up with fresh tears. 'Not again...' I mumbled to myself while subtly closing my eyes knowing...what is going to come my way.

"You never fail to make me realize how helpless I AM JOSH! STOP MAKING IT OBVIOUS!!"

Helpless... I was the same years ago when I had to watch their happiness as a couple, as legal caregivers, and as individuals slip away from my grasp and I was powerless to protect them from the harsh fate that was engulfing us.

Her voice rang throughout the house. Before I knew it, her anger episode had taken the front seat, and James' frantic wailing could be heard from the living room.

'Meredith or James? Meredith or James? Meredith or James?'

YARN – WEAVING WORDS

Illustrated by – Pratishtha Mohanty

This choice was always hard to make. Shutting my eyes close for the third time, this time it was out of frustration, and humiliation, I could feel my own anger boiling inside me of helplessness that she mentioned was the same helplessness I was facing too. We were in the same boat, but only if it was that easy to explain that to her.

"Joshie, I'm scared. I want you. Please...please come here. I'm scared. I want you, Joshie."

James' haggard voice just got louder until it was on the brink of collapsing my eardrums with its intensity.

'Meredith or James? Meredith or James? Meredith or James?'

'Inhale...exhale...inhale...and...exhale Josh.' Saying to myself, I took a deep breath amongst the loud noises surrounding me consisting of Meredith screaming all the curse words she could think of to degrade me, her anger episode reaching its peak and James weeping getting louder and louder, the way he would stutter and stumble around his words getting more audible and clearer.

Rule number two: Give the subject personal space to cool down.

And that is what I did. I held Meredith's hand, the same hands that cooked my meals when I would come home from school all tired and drenched in sweat, the same hands that would pat my back with pride whenever I would achieve something, the same hands that would massage my scalp whenever I would be stressed, the wrinkles painting her skin, I almost broke down then and there while the nostalgia of those hands and how they took care of me was hitting me like a truck, but yet again, taking a deep breath and shutting my eyes, I gently kissed her hands and left her in the room.

As I walked away into the hallway, I could hear her screams getting louder and louder, but... I had to let go. It was for the best.

Making my way towards James, I saw him clenching his plushie tightly in his arms while his whole face was covered in beads of sweat, the tears prickling at the ends of his eyes starting streaming down his cheeks as soon as my figure made its way towards him. His nose was red, the snot flowing and him sniffing loudly while the spectacles resting on his nose bridge slipped down and got hazy with the heavy breathing.

"James...Come here."

Squatting in front of him, all I had to do was plug in the earphones and play his favourite playlist of classic old poems and theme songs that children of the late 1940s played. Wrapping my arms around his slouched figure while he was sitting in a wheelchair, gently patting his back while his sniffles were starting to die down, bobbing his head to the beat of the songs, a wide smile was slowly decorating his face while his eyes were closed with ecstasy and serendipity.

If only, if only he could hear what his wife is going through in the room behind us. If only, if only he could feel how his grandson in front of him is on the brink of collapsing from exhaustion. If only she could see that the same hands, she fed me with are now invisibly choking me.

If only, it was that easy.

But...but I should hold on, remind myself yet again- priorities. Remind myself that it's not the life that matters but the courage you bring to it. Remind myself that life goes on...remind myself that someone out there needs me, Meredith and James need me.

Because I think that the heart of the connection between Meredith, James, and I has always been where my courage and will to live have always come from. Us. I treasure every memory, their input, and the blood, sweat, and tears they shed to make me who I am today.

DPS GREATER FARIDABAD

Existence is not always easy; there are ups and downs. Perhaps this is a difficult time that the three of us are meant to experience together, and the thought of our compassion is enough to make everything better. I can manage it. I will carry it out.

I admit that I was late in realizing the purpose of life and how much the two of them mean to me, but now that I am conscious of this, I am not wasting any time in showering them with nothing but unwavering love and respect.

So, I heard the sonder of my heartstrings and willed to live, gathered the courage to live for them, if not for me, I would live for them.

And once more, I tell myself that they were my glimmer of placid light when utter blackness surrounded me in my final moments.

Even though the roles have now been reversed, the bond remains the same, so once and for all, these beautiful reminders

YARN – WEAVING WORDS

of the past ingrained in my heart, spirit, and brain give me the strength that makes me stronger than ever to push through the obstacles of life and conquer this pain.

DPS GREATER FARIDABAD

ANTALE
Author: Jayati Kapur

An ardent learner, avid reader and an enthusiast, Jayati is more than just a 15-year-old student. She is attentive to her surroundings and enjoys exploring her boundaries. She aspires to leave her mark and become a role model for others to inspire them to reach the zenith. An advocate for moral values, Jayati believes in the power of love, truth and justice. Her perspective of life reflects in her writing, with which she hopes to make a difference.

ANTALE
Illustrator: Mudit Jha

Mudit really loves art with a burning passion. He doesn't really know when he started to do art but once he did start things just clicked. He got better and better and slowly but surely it transformed from a hobby to an obsession. He wants nothing more to do with his future than to earn while doing the thing he loves most: art

ANTALE
By Jayati Kapur

Here we go again...

"I am fed up. Seriously. I'm not just a forager, for Queensie's sake, I'm an explorer at heart. Can you just let me forage and explore?"

"I'm an explorer at heart", mimicked Marley, my mother dearest, "Forager Arney, escapades can be consequential. Besides, it's about more than exploring. Didn't GranAnt tell you about the scents? If you continue with this, you might end up in the death spiral."

A deafening hush followed. Mama had just said the unthinkable. My hurt features stared at her and guilt swept across her eyes as they glazed over in shame. "Honey, no, I didn't mean it that way. Look at me," she caressed my palp lovingly, "I'm just worried about you."

And rightfully so...
I revelled in the memories of my late GranAnt. Oh, how I miss her affectionate

YARN – WEAVING WORDS

call, 'Antsy Rini, there you are my peanut monster' and her loving caresses as she told me of the adventures of her and her people.

My mother's words rang in my ears, fading eventually as my mind raced with my GranAnt's warning...

Antsy Rini, have you ever wondered what happened to your grandfather, why he never returned that dark autumn night? Nobody speaks of it, for deep down, each one of us fears that death. The death your grandfather surrendered to and numerous ants before him. But you are going to be of age soon and no matter how bitter and intimidating it sounds, you must know this. That's the thing about the truth, Rini, it hurts but it must be faced.

Your grandfather, leading his army for the nth time, lost his way. The foraging party unknowingly deviated from the pheromone trail they had themselves left on their way to search for food. Our species uses pheromone trails to communicate within our colonies. The leading individual secretes pheromones, and other ants in the army have sensory organs that pick up the pheromone smell. The scouting or foraging ants leave a pheromone trail towards a secured food source for the colony to follow. But pheromones are risky.

The guiding scent of the pheromones, left just hours ago by your GrandFant, evaporated into oblivion, abandoning all those reliant on the smell. And ultimately, they ended up following each other into the Death Spiral. Round and round they went, in tiring circles, until they succumbed to exhaustion.

DEATH SPIRAL is the dark truth of our community that very few accept but it is real and no one has ever been able to break the vicious circle. When the leader loses track of the pheromones, all ants that follow, end up in a circular motion and keep following the other ants till the life begins to ebb in them.

It is heartbreaking to think of my love, out there all alone, tired, hungry and helpless. I wouldn't wish that fate upon my worst enemy. Bailey never returned. I can never forget the heavy sinking feeling in my heart, when he never barged in with his adorable excitement 'Miley, you won't believe...'.

YARN – WEAVING WORDS

The wounds so raw, so excruciating, as if it happened just yesterday. My intuition was warning me from the very beginning but I refused to listen. And now, regret has settled deep in my heart. Well, what's gone is gone. Moving on is the way of life. But that doesn't mean we mustn't learn from the experiences of our people. Remember this every step you take, there are a million ways to falter but only one to make it work. And you must make it work...

...Brushing off the memories of my GranAnt, all I did was reassure her, "You don't need to be, Mama. I'll be fine."

Was that a promise? A truth? Or a hope? None of the above. A lie, that's what it was. I wasn't going to be fine; I never was. I was a wanderer, to put it politely. And wandering never ended well. The number of times I've 'wandered' are too many for my tiny six legs to count. And that was only when I was supposed to follow a Senior.

However, things were liable to change, to think of shouldering responsibilities was a different matter altogether. I was old enough and more than ready.

Finally. I was no longer an InfAnt, trailing behind my mother, always sheltered in her shadow, sheltered from life. Rather, I was now an Ant, an independent grown-up Ant.

Which meant I now go on my first official Raid at the forefront. I was going to FINALLY lead my army. My Sepoys, as I'd christened them. I was so excited. Mama had so many expectations from me and so did the entire clan.

Yet, doubt intimidated me and dampened my fierce confidence. It was a different thing to forage and loose my way, pheromones were going to save me eventually or Mama Marley. But Mama won't be there. I had to scout. I had to leave my pheromone trail. I had to marshal my Sepoys to safety. All the while managing not to get distracted and plummet us all to death. It was a different thing to fend for oneself and an entirely different thing to shoulder the weight of an army, all alone.

YARN – WEAVING WORDS

The latter was much more terrifying, trust me.

I looked towards my friends, future Sepoys, basking in the dull shiver of the night sky, chirping loudly. Louder and louder and louder, until happy chitters were interrupted by angry ones. The buzz kills were at it again. Adult ants disbanded the congregation, issuing a decree for the giggling gang to drift off to sleep. Wishes for the night were exchanged with tickles to the palp. Oh, how I love my palp, expresses what the chirps can't, describes what the eyes fail to. The pair of elongated appendages protruding near the mouth, associated with touch and taste, what we call the palp. We ants communicate via the palp, the human equivalent of a sensory organ. A single touch, and a story is told.

I sat huddled in my refuge (location shall not be divulged for privacy reasons). I relived the time Queensie called me over. Her words will always stick by me and give me the push I lack or the embrace I yearn.

DPS GREATER FARIDABAD

Don't let the brilliance of your instincts and the glimmer of hope in your eyes ever extinguish. When everything fades away and you feel alone, remember yourself. Your courage and the power of the scents are your greatest assets. No human infestation can stop you; no predator can get to you if you exude confidence. Don't forget the oaths of the colony and the promise to your kind. You are young, full of life, yet to see the world in its true colours. Life isn't always food, family or foraging. It's way more, and while that might intimidate you, it is the truth. And that's just the thing about truth.

As a Queen, I must shelter the colony and stand resilient, infrangible and valiant. But as a fellow ant, I can admit, it wasn't always easy. I had my fair share of insecurities and apprehensions.

I was always destined to be the Queen. As the custom is, the Queen has to leave the clan and move away to start her own lineage, write her own destiny. But leaving the colony and with it, my life, family and every comfort I had ever known asked for a strength of will and endurance to sacrifice and conquer my apprehension. But I triumphed and emerged victorious. So shall you.

YARN – WEAVING WORDS

Illustrated by – Mudit Jha

Queensie's words faded in my thoughts as I became conscious of my surroundings and with the comfort of her reassurance, I resolved to not lose hope and retired for the day.

We started out well enough, passing on our way a multitude of sights. On a normal occasion where I'd be following a Senior, I might never have appreciated the majestic marvels to behold. We gradually exited the fresh air of the lucid evening sky, glittering with sincerity, entering the occluded passages.

The soft comfort of the earth of the garden suddenly metamorphosed into hard cold flooring of the building, the clean scents of recently turned dirt turning to the sharp odour of civilization. The familiarity of well traversed paths was replaced with an awe for the unknown surroundings. My mind strived to chronicle the landmarks to ensure an easy return.

I distinctly remember the creepy spider, empty eyes staring into nothing and legs

YARN – WEAVING WORDS

sprawled, that I sneakily avoided, I had enough on my plate as is. The colloidal rock was where we'd stopped for a jiffy so I could roughly head count my Sepoys. And then we carried on, exiting the natural landscapes that gave way to the human settlement (still an infestation for me. Pests, that's what they were, the lot!)

The wooden flooring, brilliant incandescence and enormous columns left me agape in a soft fiery flush. Tangible figurines, towering platforms and alien articles, or might I say, landmarks for our voyage back, decorated the scene. I noticed in particular the peculiar looking stick, with protrusions on the side and attractive in design. A tip bulged from one end while the other was obscure to my vision.

The gorgeous ornaments we passed, forever etched in my memory, their beauty absolute and unflinching. Another peculiarity that caught my interest was the silken garment that mesmerized me with its unique texture, like nothing I had seen before.

DPS GREATER FARIDABAD

The thundering steps shook me to the core. Look at those giant boulders wreaking destruction in their wake. And to think they call them feet. I jinx the wretched devil to hurt its toes on a piece of–

Aaaaaaaaaahhhhhhh!!! A human bellowed in pain. That was quick. Why didn't I demand for an infinite supply of peanut butter?

Well, in my personal opinion, their so-called feet aren't even legitimate. Feet are those that I have, beautiful, six in number but just enough. Their incompetent two feet must be useless. That reminds me of my next landmark, the colossal shoe. It was a work of art but improper for the Homosapien it belonged to.

And finally, we decided to turn back. Each detail of the setting we encountered will stay by me till time immemorial.

Our findings were more than satisfactory- A mountain of bread, two sugar volcanos, a giant pool of peanut butter (my personal

YARN – WEAVING WORDS

favorite of the lot) and the cake plateau. I had competently marshaled my Sepoys, found large sources of food, even in the dangerous territory, completely infested with humans. (A professional advice, human infestations are where all the good stuff is!)

We made our way back to the colony, satisfied with our findings. But something changed. Did I get distracted again? Was it the dead spider from the species I feared? Or the giant Boulder or the massive tarpaulin I had avoided on the way. The cause was no longer important. Bottom line was I took a wrong turn and that's all it took.

I was lost. Again. This time however, I couldn't follow a fellow to safety. I was at the forefront and I had caused this. The faint pheromones against the backdrop of my fear became fainter and fainter. The trail was going cold. The haemolymph (puny humans call it blood, duh!) in my haemocoels (just like veins and arteries in the silly human species) chilled to an unnerving degree. Every forager's worst nightmare was gradually becoming my reality.

I was in the Death Spiral and so was my army. And I might as well have murdered my Sepoys in cold blood. No one had ever survived this before. Why, oh why, dear Queen must this happen to me of all ants!

How I knew I was in the death spiral? Well, I'm pretty sure I was supposed to lead the army and not follow another. At that moment however, I was doing exactly that. If I was following someone who was following someone else and so on and so forth, essentially, we were all just following each other. No, no, no, this was NOT supposed to happen. Apocalypse was coming, I could feel it.

A million thoughts ran in my head that very instant. All my dreams, hopes of success and being lauded by Mama and the colony, crumbled to dust in an instant. I had to do something. What? How? When? Questions

YARN – WEAVING WORDS

bombarded me along with fear that exponentially grew every second.

Everything stilled. Like life skidded to a stop. All but my beating heart and loud crushing steps. Every ounce of my being was alert and aware. My mind cleared and gave way to actual contemplation. And then it hit me bitter in the face. I had to stop. Every step counts, even the ones we don't take. And I stopped. A Sepoy bumped into me and the army collided into one another to a confused halt.

The gears inside worked overtime as a plan unfolded itself. We had some food, hopefully enough to thrive on for just long enough. And I distinctly remembered each landmark, the spider, the rock, the coloured stick, the cloth and lastly, the giant shoe of the puny human who tried to squish me.

All I had to do was trace the marks backwards and find the dying trail. A touch to the palp of each of my buddies informed the army that we were lost. The frightened chitters and angry chirps took a while to calm. But they got the message eventually - I would be off on my own until I secured the trail.

The food, as little as it was in quantity, was to be used judiciously. And lastly, nobody moved until I returned.
I appointed second in line to me, Barney, as the leader. Holding onto the small helping of peanut sauce I'd found, I left my anxious Sepoys.

I strode towards nowhere in particular, wondering if I was lost for good and would meet my demise in this miserable fashion. But, by the grace of the Queen, found my second landmark, the fascinating stick. This had been the fourth mark on our way out. (the shoe, the fifth, was suddenly nowhere to be found. And this is exactly why I don't trust the human pests. They probably ate the giant shoe. Pathetic.)

My gut propelled to keep going in directions I wouldn't have fathomed had I been in control. Luckily for me, I was not, almost, like I had been possessed.

I trudged on, passing the cloth and boulder uneventfully. My tiny legs became weary with each step I took, but the confidence I felt in my gait, was renewed and strengthened every second as I felt myself drawing closer and closer to my next milestone.

And then I saw it. My next milestone. Uh oh.

The dead spider was no less terrifying in its lifeless form but the hovering mourner was what sealed the deal for my death. My history with spiders goes back a long way, but that's a story for another day. For the time being, I focused on my grieving predator.

In some safely tucked away part of my heart, I felt a tinge of sympathy for the grief-stricken spider but my overwhelming fear took the better of me. I regarded the pair with contempt, forgetting at the moment, the beings' suffering. My heart pounded against my chest and I felt each throb against my ears in the deafening silence of the distressed twilight. With shaking legs and murmurs of consolation from deep within, I trudged the short marathon to the monsters, step after step. My six legs each trembled, not from my weight but that of my fear.

Looking neither left nor right, I walked on and on. Yet as I drew nearer to my greatest fear, time stilled a second time. My profound heartbeat was accompanied with a fresh reverberation growing louder and louder. Soft sobs. I looked towards the departed and its partner.

And I began to question the gravity of my fear, was it even real? I walked, dazed, towards my once greatest fear and with a soft touch of my leg to his, I embraced a mourning soul. The spider looked over at my insignificant self, a being much smaller than him. But all I saw was a bittersweet gratefulness in his broken eyes. Leaving a drop of my peanut delicacy as a sign of respect, I went on.

YARN – WEAVING WORDS

It was at this moment that I realized something that has stuck by me forever. Fear is a perception. And there is much more beyond the shackles of trepidation. In that thought was solace, was there not?

A satisfaction of an insignificant victory, over my fear, settled in my heart and I moved on, more valiant and composed than ever.

And ultimately, home. But the escapade was long from its end. I had to seek help. I felt a qualm and questioned myself for a brief moment, imagining the disappointment at my mother's face and the colony's punctured faith. But, seeking help isn't a sign of weakness, rather a celebration of fraternity and trust. And one must never regret asking for guidance whenever necessary. And so, I reached out.

As I saw my mother, tears welled up in my eyes. The colony gathered around me as I narrated my solitary adventure. The elders listened patiently, formulated a search party and set out. I had messed up and I knew it. But my elders had faith in me and put me at the forefront of the search party, setting an enormous responsibility on my tiny shoulders. It is one thing to err, and another to rise from it. But rising above our faltered steps needs validation and motivation from those that matter. The faith endowed in me that day by the colony can never equal any support I needed.

With renewed confidence, I worked my way through the same landmarks but this time with the support of my entire family. It wasn't long before we found my abandoned army of Sepoys. All was well. The excited chitters of praise overwhelmed me and I began to cry, more from relief than happiness. We made our way back to the colony, safe and secure. Shortly, we treaded the same path that had once induced horrors but also learnings that would last a lifetime. Food was secured and my escapade finally concluded with an optimistic and hopeful end.

I had conquered my fears and emerged victorious. I comprehended a truth I had

YARN – WEAVING WORDS

been deprived of all this while: We manifest Fear and Courage in our lives as we perceive them. It is important to understand – *'It is not life that matters but the courage we bring to it.'*

DPS GREATER FARIDABAD

The Red Bag
Author: Pakhi Arora

Pakhi Arora is a 15-year-old budding author. She is a keen learner and loves reading books. She has an interest in sketching and likes dancing. The theme of the story contemplates the reader to inculcate courage in one's life and give it meaning.

YARN – WEAVING WORDS

The Red Bag
Illustrator: Rishit Mittal

Rishit is a 15-year-old student of class IX from Delhi Public School Greater Faridabad. He spends most of his free time sketching and creating new illustrations. He loves reading books as they help him think creatively. He is a perfectionist who works on minute details to bring his art alive.

DPS GREATER FARIDABAD

The Red Bag
By Pakhi Arora

"Venu, why are you weeping? What's the matter?". "Sahab ji, the doctor has told my mother that her heart needs to be operated as soon as possible to save her life, but I don't have any money." "It's ok Venu, I will try to do what I can." Rishi was working at his office till late when Venu, a tea seller, brought tea for him.

His moist eyes reflected the deep sorrow in his heart. After completing his work, Rishi got up from his chair to go. "Let's go have some Vada pav, it's been a long time since we haven't enjoyed the snack at the Foodies," suggested Rishi's colleagues.

Tired of his dull routine, this suggestion seemed to be a welcome break even though he knew Pooja would be waiting for him for dinner. Also, he could not help but only think about Venu, his teary-eyed face flashing before his eyes. How his own mother's face flashed before his eyes, though she lived in the village on the family farm, he hardly met her once a year, he could not imagine never being able to see her ever again. He missed his mother's warm loving caress on his forehead and probably this made him more empathetic towards Venu. Rishi shrugged off his thoughts and accompanied his friends to the nearby kiosk of Foodies to have Vada pav.

"Venu urgently needs money for his mother's operation, and he's really concerned about her as she's the only person in his life who made him look up to the world, he could't lose her, I think we should help him financially also we should go meet her in the hospital," recommended Rishi to his friends. "Yes, we can start collecting funds for her as soon as possible," said one of them. "Ok then, I'll go now, Pooja is waiting for me for dinner."

Thinking about the importance of a mother in one's life, Rishi went to his car after eating. His gaze fell upon a red-colored bag lying on the busy road. He picked it up and tried to scrutinize it. He was curious to see what was inside and decided to unzip it. "Hey, don't touch that bag, it may contain something dangerous or an explosive that could harm you," warned his friend. He looked around for the owner of the bag, but he couldn't find anyone. He left the bag on the roadside for the owner to come and take it from where he had lost it and went back home.

He was tired after a whole day of hard work and was propped on the bed, scrolling his phone. He was thinking about that bag, what might have been inside it...if the bag reached the person who might have lost it or not. Lots of thoughts flooded his mind and with thousands of mysteries and problems.

"What happened? You're looking worried." "Nothing much Pooja, just a stressful day, and I got reminded of Maa, thinking about Venu's mother." "Don't worry, we'll go to meet her next Sunday in the village, and what about Venu's mom?" "She has to get her operation done but how can a tea seller

YARN – WEAVING WORDS

afford such expenses." "God will surely find a way to help Venu's mom, you would be tired, let's go to sleep now," said Pooja.

The next day, he got ready for work and went to his car. He saw the same, red-coloured bag that he had seen the previous night. He was stunned to see that again. "How come this bag keeps coming back to me? I think I should check what's in there."

He opened the bag and saw that it was full of money. What an irony! Here someone has left so much money by mistake and there Venu is in desperate need for it. He went back home to tell Pooja about this. "You should check it properly, maybe we get any clue about whose money is it," she suggested. They unpacked the whole bag of money on the table and found a torn visiting card and a letter.

The visiting card had the name, 'Srinivas Kumar' on it but the phone number wasn't visible. "Let's open the letter, maybe we get an idea." "No Rishi, it's not right to open someone's personal letter, it could be related to some confidential matter. Maybe we can find Srinivas Kumar's number on social media." They both started to search for him, and they found three accounts with the same names.

They called all three of them but sadly everyone claimed the lost money was theirs. They were confused who the real owner of the money was. So, they thought of a plan to find who was the rightful owner of the bag.

Rishi called all the three of them to meet him at his home, first at 6:00 pm, second at 6:15, and third at 6:30.

They both were eagerly waiting for them to come and hoping that the money reaches the right person. Rishi was preparing himself and finally, it was time! The bell rang, and a man 6'ft tall wearing a black suit with black-rimmed spectacles, he looked like a big businessman and his eyes searched for the bag, little did he know that he would have to answer a few questions before taking his bag.

YARN – WEAVING WORDS

Illustrated by Rishit Mittal

"Welcome sir, I have your bag of money which you might have lost yesterday". "Oh yes! thanks a lot, these days, no one is as loyal as you, everyone is greedy and never returns money."

He came inside and sat on the off-white sofa where Pooja was staring at him, trying to know his intentions. I will give you that bag on one condition, you'll have to answer my question".
"Yes sure, go ahead."
"So, what was the colour of that bag?" he asked.
"Umm, it was blue" he stuttered.
"Are you sure? Because the one I have is a yellow-coloured bag."
"Yes, yes! It could be yellow too; I have forgotten the colour."
He clearly was panic-stricken and sweat dripped off his face which made Rishi sure that he wasn't the one he was looking for.
"Ok sir, you will have to wait inside for some time if you want your bag."

It was time for the second person to come in and Rishi had hoped that the person would be the owner. The other one was a casual man with a beard and the confidence in his eyes was a sigh for Rishi. "Thank you, Mr. Rishi, I had collected that money for my sister's wedding, and it got lost, and now because of you, I can have the money back," he said. "Yes, but before that, can I ask you one question?". "Yes sure, you can." "How much money was there inside your bag?". "There were around 20 lakhs". "But I have counted, it had 10 lakhs." Oh yes, sorry, I had given 5 lakhs to my friend.

Rishi gave him a suspicious look and now there was no hope for the second one too as it was clear the man did not know how much money was there in the bag. He was really concerned and prayed that the third person was the real Srinivas Kumar.

Both were sitting in an adjacent room and Rishi was eagerly waiting for the third one to come but he didn't show up. The other people lost their temper and started fighting for the bag. "Rishi please give me my bag; he is fake and wants to take my money". "Now the cops will decide who is fake and who is real," said Rishi. Both the men who claimed to be the Srinivas he was looking for were caught up in a frenzy of fear. The greed for the money got them into great misery which now made them disown the same bag which they claimed was theirs. They ran back through the same beige door from which they entered.

Rishi was still in dilemma and started thinking of another idea with his wife to find the real owner. He decided to open the letter which was in the bag to see because there was no other option left. It was a fine piece of paper with a message written in blue ink. It said –

Dear recipient,
"I had a good life and a loving family but one day, three years ago, I lost everything and everyone in an unfortunate incident, and eventually lost my business too. I had to sell my house and all the property, I was literally on the road and had no money left even to eat a day's meal. There was no hope...but miracles do happen. I was sitting on a grey pavement along the roadside looking at the

YARN – WEAVING WORDS

cars passing by. I saw a red bag lying far from me. I went closer to have a good look and asked the nearby vegetable vendor if he knew whose it was but he had no idea about it. I unzipped it and to my amazement, it was full of money.

I tried to find out whose bag it was but no one claimed it so I decided to keep it as a loan from God and if someone ever claimed the bag, I would return the money with interest eventually when I will earn enough. I had forgotten the thought of giving up on life after getting that money and decided to put that money into the start-up business and luckily, I earned a lot of profit. Gradually my life became more sorted, and I had a well-settled business after around six months.

I could never find out whose mystery bag it was. Since then, I keep the same amount of money every year, on the same day, for a needy person. At least I can save a life every year like someone's money saved mine. If you have found the bag and if you are not so needy, then please give it to someone who

really needs it. I already give charity but I put this mysterious bag as I feel that it's the mystery of life that sometimes destiny makes you find the bag and sometimes the bag finds you.
– From Srinivas Kumar".

"Wow! What a great thought! Rishi what will you do with this money," inquired Pooja. "I know what I have to do." Rishi dashed to his office but did not enter the building, rather he went to the side lane near his office and met Venu. "You didn't have money for your mother's operation, here take this money. I hope it will be enough". "Thank you so much Sahab ji, I will never be able to repay your debt." "Don't worry, keep it as a gift from God."

After few hours, Rishi got a call from an unknown number.

"Hello, who is this?"

"You know enough about me already. I was at your home yesterday. I am the first

YARN – WEAVING WORDS

Srinivas Kumar you had met, the one who was once poor but that bag saved me."

"Oh, so you lied yesterday about the colour of the bag?"

"Yes, I did, I came to your house because I wanted to know if my red bag got into the right hands or not."

DPS GREATER FARIDABAD

Fortitude
Author: **Nysa Mishra**

Nysa Mishra, born in Delhi, is a 14-year-old budding writer. Nysa considers her faith and family to be the most important to her. If she isn't spending time with her friends and family, one can almost always find her buried in her books. She aspires to become a doctor in future and pursue her interest in science.

Fortitude
Illustrator: Rishit Mittal

Rishit is a 15-year-old student of class IX from Delhi Public School Greater Faridabad. He spends most of his free time sketching and creating new illustrations. He loves reading books as they help him think creatively. He is a perfectionist who works on minute details to bring his art alive.

DPS GREATER FARIDABAD

Fortitude
By Nysa Mishra

Strapping on her bag, Alisha was ready. After putting much thought into it, she was ready to climb Mount Everest. Alisha dreamed of reaching the peak of heaven since she was a kid. Ignoring all the deterrence of her relatives and friends, she decided to move on to fulfill her dream.

After a trek for seven days, she reached the South Base Camp in Nepal. It is located at an altitude of 5364 feet. Glancing at her surroundings, she was shocked to see the Mountain's glory. The phantom-white mountain reared into the sky, a glorious sight in the dead of winter. The extremely cold weather and sub-zero temperature made her shiver even in her several layers of warm clothing. She started wearing her climbing gear, took a deep breath, and as always prayed to Lord Jagannath for her safe journey and started her expedition.
She saw a man at a distance who seemed to be climbing the mountain too and went up to him. She asked the man kindly, "Excuse

me sir, are you also planning to climb that mountain?" She could not decipher the expression on the old man's face. The man answered, "Oh! That mountain is one of the most difficult one to climb. Many people have given up halfway. Looking at you it seems you too want to climb that mountain. Child, are you sure of your decision?" With a smile, she nodded. She did not want to communicate about her fervor and determination about climbing Everest.

She remembered the times her father convinced her to be a doctor just because he saw the potential in her to become one. They would often end up fighting, her father ending up in his room sulking about the fact that he could not convince his daughter and she in hers hoping that he would understand her passion one day. More than her passion, it was her mission to prove her worth to the world.

She was determined to climb that mountain.

DPS GREATER FARIDABAD

The monotony of the trek towards the base camp refreshed her memory of an incident. It was daunting. *"Bhabhi, I am telling you. Fix this girl's marriage."* was her aunt's word to her mom. *Alisha had told her family about her career choice but her parents disapproved as they wanted her to be a doctor and become independent.*

Her relatives too spurned this idea. "She will end up nowhere with this stupid hobby of hers. What is the point of wasting so much money on her? It is just a phase. She will grow out of it soon. In the end, she only has to take care of her kids and husband. Listen to me and teach her how to cook. My brother's son is unmarried. He is a software engineer and earns a lot of money. We are looking for a girl just like our Alisha. If you want, I can set up their marriage."

Alisha was furious at what her aunt said but her parents assured her not to worry. They wanted her to become a doctor and had no intention of getting her married soon. Alisha studied hard to not only fulfil her dream but also to prove what she is capable of.

YARN – WEAVING WORDS

She sighed heavily, letting her head drop. A single tear rolled down her cheek. These past four months were treacherous owing to the condemnation she faced. Her parents were forcing her to prepare for the medical entrance exam. They believed that Alisha had the potential to be an affable doctor.

Taking a sip of warm water, she sat down. Five hours had passed. She looked up. She had not even covered half of the mountain. She had reached Camp II. Climbing to Camp II did not involve substantial technical difficulties, but it indeed demanded a high level of proficiency on steep and exposed terrain at high altitudes. Tiredness washed over her eyes. Her muscles felt sore. She almost wanted to give up but then she remembered her aunt's words.

Anger surged through her veins as she remembered all the criticism she and her parents had to bear. There were times when she used to have big breakdowns at night in her room. She used to cradle herself to sleep while the tears stained her pillow thinking about all the derogatory comments. She used to think of herself as dismayed. She remembered the punitive words of her father, *"You will not go to that wretched Uttarkashi Institute of Mountaineering!!"* It hurts her to think that her father was irked by the fact that his only daughter wanted to follow her dreams and opt for mountaineering rather than taking up a lucrative career.

Enraged by his daughter, he threw a plate at her feet. It shattered into a million pieces just like her heart, resulting in the shards piercing her. She yelped in pain and quietly went to her room. Her eyes grew hot, the tears welling so quickly that it was impossible to blink them away. She choked on a small but audible sob. "Why is it always me?" She sobbed quietly, engulfing all the pain and anger of her father.

She got up with all her strength and continued her journey. After a very arduous trek of few hours, Alisha made it to South Col. Her instructor told her that South Col was the most difficult trek due to

YARN – WEAVING WORDS

Illustrated by - Rishit Mittal

it being the coldest spot in the world at a height of 7906 meters from the sea level. The co-climbers of her trekking expedition congratulated her as it was her first climb. All others were more experienced and acclimatized. Most people gave up before reaching till this point as it was a tough terrain especially on their first attempt. Reaching here meant that the rest is doable. The winds had grown stronger and the clouds hovering were an indication that they should return to camp II for the night in time. They would go further till the next and final camp the next day.

Everyone started moving, but Alisha did not. She wanted to soak in the significance of this moment in her life, of living this success. She told everyone that she needed few minutes by herself and would join them and that they should go ahead. Giving her those few minutes did not seem too dangerous, so everyone left.

Alisha closed her eyes, taking in a deep breath but this time her aunt, her father, those harsh words, nothing flashed before her like always. This time, the view of the white mountains flashed before her eyes, where she was.

Another memory ran across her mind. It was about the best decision she could ever take. It was when her father did not support her decision of taking up mountaineering. *Wiping her tears, she stood up against all odds with courage and faith in herself, all the more determined to scale Mt Everest. She knew that in order to fulfill her dream and achieve success, she will have to work for it. Sprinting to her bed, she pulled out her laptop. Her fingers took her to job application sites. She decided that she would work part time and pay her fees at the Uttarkashi Mountaineering Institute. Luckily, she got an online tutoring job for students living abroad. This job was sure to give her around thirty thousand rupees per month.*

"Finally, I will be able to initiate my journey of becoming a mountaineer", Alisha penned her thoughts in her diary. She further confided in it of her several mountaineering

expeditions which she undertook while getting trained at the Uttarkashi's institute.

After successfully climbing Stok Kangri (a 6000 m trekking peak in Ladakh), Alisha knew she was ready for an expedition to Everest. But she needed something more than physical endurance and mental toughness and that was a whopping 30 lakh rupees to bask in the glory of reaching the summit of the mountain. She slept on her desk after writing in her diary, "How will I be able to raise funds? Should I knock the doors of government buildings, get crowd-funded or get sponsored by a rich businessman?"

Her father saw her sleeping with her head on the desk and quietly took her diary to glance through what she had written. It was then that he realized how earnestly Alisha wanted to pursue her dream and finally decided to help her realize her dream by sponsoring her expedition. Alisha hugged him tightly and could hardly speak anything when she found her father stand by her. Her happiness knew no bounds.

YARN – WEAVING WORDS

Time had paused for her today as she found herself literally on top of the world. She devoured everything with her eyes and apparently wanted to capture the immensity of the moment by clicking a few photographs and started her journey back to join her crew at the camp. The bitter cold harsh winds were piercing into her wheatish skin. Suddenly her breath became convulsed. She gasped for air as she fell into a crevasse.

Terror plastered her face, and she was getting dizzy. With a thud, she fell on the mound of snow. Her wheatish complexion now turned pale, making her frostnip stand out. Her eyes became droopy. Her entire life flashed before her eyes. All her birthdays, the lovely times she spent with her friends and family, and the struggle she faced all came back to her and along with it her sweet success.

Suddenly, everything became black. No movement, no sounds, only the harsh blowing winds. Alisha lost all her senses. Her lips tugged into a small smile when she looked at the stretch of white mountains one last time. Her eyes slowly closing as she drifted into a deep slumber.

She was happy about what all she had accomplished till now and embraced her demise with valour. She was finally on her way to the peak of heaven...

***

Folding the newspaper, Alisha's father had a proud smile on his face, though his eyes showed sadness. His only daughter had made him proud. He went back to Alisha's room. The room still smelt like the peony perfume she wore. He remembered how he used to call his daughter a flower because of her natural, sweet scent.

He picked up a photo from the table. It was his picture with Alisha which was clicked when she was five. A single tear rolled down his cheek on to the photo frame realizing that he could never see his daughter. Caressing her photo and recalling her last glimpse, he remembered the smile on her frozen face, an assurance that she lived her last moments in the bliss of her achievement. He murmured, "You made me realize that TIME is just an illusion and the most precious moment to embrace is 'NOW'. In focusing more on the past or future or fulfilling our expectations we miss the 'NOW.' I would never have the courage you had to climb that mountain. I love you my little flower. I would sell my soul for a minute to see you. Until we meet again in eternity."

Most people in the crowd are happy with what they find easy. They never think that they have the potential to achieve more. Even people who are not happy, do not want to take any risks. They think if they take risks, they will lose what they already have. But to reach a new peak, we need to put in our effort. Many of them do not show any courage, and they remain part of the crowd their whole life. They keep complaining about the handful of courageous people and call them lucky. Never have regrets in your life and live each moment as if it were the last.

DPS GREATER FARIDABAD

The Courage She Had
Author: Lavanya Mittal

Lavanya studies in class IX. She is a passionate amateur writer who is always curious about the world around, and tends to question everything and wants to know about it. She is contemplative in nature. She feels intrigued with the purpose of life and wishes to makes the world a better place.

YARN – WEAVING WORDS

The Courage She Had
Illustrator: Sehar Yadav

Sehar is 14 years old studying in IX class. She has a panache for drawing and loves creating sketches. She aspires to be an entrepreneur. She also enjoys reading books and writing.

The Courage She Had
By Lavanya Mittal

Standing on the terrace balustrade remembering all the pain and suffering she had been through and recalling what the cruel fate has done to her, she closed her eyes, and all the painful memories came flooding of the day her happy life changed forever.

Priya and her father shared a very deep connection. He was the world to her. Priya's father was a pilot by profession and being close to him, she always wanted to make him proud.

2:30 am, when the world slept peacefully, Priya's father, as always got dressed for his flight from Delhi to Mumbai. She loved to see him in his uniform and would make sure to wake up to say goodbye. While departing from the house, Priya's father hugged her and said, "Bye Priyu, I will be back soon, study hard."

"I love you too papa! Come back soon!"

YARN – WEAVING WORDS

After he left, Priya told her mother "Mumma I miss papa when will he come back? I don't feel good." Priya's mom comforted her and said, "Don't worry dear, Papa will be back soon. Everything is fine, come and let's sleep." She lay down beside her, closed her eyes and happy moments flashed across her mind bringing a smile to her face. Then she sank into a sonorous slumber.

A few hours later the plane encountered turbulence. Priya's father tried his best to make a safe landing, but the engines stopped due to a technical issue the plane crashed near the Mumbai Airport in the sea. The pilot's cabin received most of the damage. Medics and safety boats reached the place as soon as possible. Most passengers were alive except the ones who were close to the pilot's cabin.

But unfortunately, Priya's father couldn't survive; he drowned in the sea even though he knew swimming but due to head injury, he could not gather courage to keep himself afloat.

7:30 am, the phone rang, "Hello ma'am, is this pilot Akshat's wife?"
"Yes, it is me"
"The flight 467 from Delhi to Mumbai crashed in the sea. I am sorry, but your husband could not make it. Can you please come to the office in Delhi for all the official procedures?"

The words echoed in Smriti's ears as she heard about her husband's ill-fated flight. The world went black. She had to think quickly. She gathered herself and told Priya that she was going for some work and rushed to the office. Holding back her tears, she completed paperwork. The manager of the department said, "We are sorry for your loss, ma'am," Priya's mother reached home and with a heavy heart informed Priya about her father's death. Priya's feelings slowly crept in as she could see nothing around her. Tears streamed her eyes. Hugging her mother, she cried for hours.

Next day was the toughest one for all. Priya burst into tears after seeing her father's corpse. Clouds hid the afternoon sun and the sky became melancholic. Priya refused to eat or drink. She spent days and nights sitting hugging her father's photo in the hope that it was a wild dream and everything would be fine when she will wake up.

Almost two years passed, Priya was still in severe depression and suffered from anxiety. Smriti, was now the earning member in the family. She worked in a small firm for their survival but it could hardly make ends meet. She kept all her suffering and struggle concealed behind a smile just for the sake of Priya. She tried her best but could not help her come out of depression and anxiety.

One bright spring day, Smriti decided to take her to a picnic. It was like a victory for her as she saw her daughter smile and talk, forgetting her father's absence for a while. Priya's laughter made her forget her own pain and struggle. The sun shone bright, pushing away all the darkness and gloominess in her heart and making her life a bit brighter while coming back.

This happiness was too short lived. While driving back they met with a fatal accident. Priya's mother died on the spot because of excess bleeding. Priya suffered major injuries, her bones were crushed and she went into a coma. Police admitted her to the government hospital, where she regained consciousness but it took her months to recover.

Priya became completely silent, and her life looked as if she had nothing left in it, no place to go, no one to talk to. Priya's mother was the only daughter in her family and her father had an older sister but she refused to take responsibility for Priya. The so-called relatives had decided to distance themselves as much as they could. Orphanage was her new home and she was part of group of 150 orphaned children, Hunger became a part of her life and so was misery. The girl who was pampered by her parents had to work by cleaning up the place.

YARN – WEAVING WORDS

Illustrated by Sehar Yadav

After completing that day's work, while standing on the terrace balustrade, she remembered all the pain and suffering she had been through and recalled what her cruel fate had done to her. She closed her eyes, and all the painful memories came flooding.

She decided to end all the pain forever as she was about to step forward. She took a deep breath and said to herself, "I can't die right now; I have to live and make my Papa's dream come true. My mother didn't raise a coward, she raised a fighter." Priya resisted all the pain and cried till she had no more tears left.

From that day she worked hard, completed her studies and learned to code. All her hard work and dedication paid off when she won a scholarship for higher studies in the USA with all her expenses paid. She completed her BTech. in Computer Science and got a job in a very good company. She worked there for a year and a half understanding the industry.

YARN – WEAVING WORDS

Her ambition to become an entrepreneur led her to look for investors. After a few months of struggle, she moved on to establish her E-commerce website Mango which dealt in luxurious brands, but it failed. Slowly she ran out of money and the company shut down. But she didn't give up. She spent all her savings to return her loans and went on to study Business Management on scholarship and chiseled her entrepreneurial skills.

After few years of struggling with different jobs, she managed to get a few partners to start a new business. She provided solutions based on Artificial Intelligence which could detect errors in major machinery like factory machines, construction cranes, railway etc. that changed society for the better. One of her projects was to detect errors in planes that could stop accidents by eighty percent.

Her hard work paid off, and in the end, she made frequent television appearances and became a world-renowned entrepreneur. She won multiple awards fulfilling her father's dream she got featured in the Forbes list and ended up building a great life for herself with her hard work. Still, the cause of her father's death was a mystery.

Priya worked with the airlines where her father worked. Her profile included ways to enhance the performance of planes with tech support. Nobody recognized the little orphaned girl, Priya. Soon, she made friends with employees who had access to old records she looked through old records every day until she found out why her father's plane crashed.

Was it due to a technical issue which was the company's fault?
She discovered that the airlines never replaced old planes due to which the engines failed. She also found that it wasn't the first time that such an accident had occurred. It had happened five times in the past few years, but the company management was so good at hiding that no one ever got to know. She sued the company for all of the things they did, and

the company had to shut down and pay heavy compensation to the victims.

She bought the airlines her father used to work in. and she always made sure for the flights to be extra secure although she could not bring her father back and change the past she made sure no one suffered the way she did. She also wrote her biography named *'Sahas'* (Hindi word for courage.) which became a bestseller.

With all the money she received as compensation, she opened an orphanage where no one suffered the way she did. The orphan children lived like a family, and they didn't have to work. Special attention was given to the mental health of children. Priya's work got recognized by UNICEF and she got invited to UNICEF to give a speech. In the end, she realized it's not a life that matters but the courage you put into it. In the end, she made it due to her courage.

DPS GREATER FARIDABAD

Jewels in the Eyes
Author: Attrija Abhijit Gitay

Attrija wishes to expose the hidden and forgotten tidbits of colourful emotions and the beauty in human vulnerability through her writings, with a special focus on individuality and honouring one's journey rhus allowing her to unearth the complexities of human lives, by finding the mundane clues and revelations that lead her to secret doors and beyond. She has always been a voracious reader. Her favourite poet is Sylvia Plath. She loves classic literature, poetry, Renaissance art, stoicism, theology, politics and history.

YARN – WEAVING WORDS

Jewels in the Eyes
Illustrator: Saara Gaur

Saara Gaur, a humanities student who sees life as an adventure. Her obsession with helps her bring out her skills and prowess on canvas. She works with her hands and draws from her heart with lots of experiences that are set into an uncommon panorama. Apart from her artistic disposition, she is also inclined towards indie-rock music, movies, books and traveling.

DPS GREATER FARIDABAD

Jewels in the Eyes
"Kaleidoscope of memories"
By Attrija Gitay

I tried to sleep under the purple iridescent lights and loud commotion of voices in the aeroplane but all I could see behind the darkness of my closed eyes was a kaleidoscope of memories. Aeroplanes have always been a place of meditation for me, even in the backdrop of a deafening sound of the whir of the wings. There was nothing that I wanted to do other than go back home again.

It had been my first trip home after years. College life in Czechia kept me on my toes for so long that I learnt how to not miss home. Nevertheless, I don't wish to whine because it was a privilege to live a life I had always dreamt of. Czechia was the magic lamp of my wishes. I knew from the beginning that I was meant to be there. The highs and troughs of colours of the houses, buildings and nature made me feel alive and accomplished. How could I not want to live there forever?

YARN – WEAVING WORDS

Despite some minor and major twists, it was *beautiful.*

It wasn't right, though, to forget home. Something needed to be done. A time machine, appearing out of nowhere at this point, would have changed a lot of things…….

"Melting hands of time"
I saw a little girl of ten, dressed in a turquoise and burgundy pinafore dress, walking, and touching everything that she liked, murmuring a quiet prayer. Her touch had always been like that of *Midas* but she had casually been unaware of it. There was a chic elegance in the way she walked. I decided to follow her because there was something about her that didn't let me ignore her demeanour.

She was not aware of my presence at first, allowing her to be her authentic-self under the shadow of an unknown person. She was so mindful of every little thing that I struggled to even fathom her saintliness at such a young age. I admired how she caressed her own face, softly slid her hair behind her ears and gathered her thoughts. I do understand, my dear reader, that you might be thinking about my observations about her from such a long distance; I didn't need to try to observe her, it was stark clear, even though she didn't look back.

I got lost in my thoughts and lost track of her speed. She was now walking faster than me. I wanted to run behind her but it would have pushed her further away from me.
Could I have known her next stop? Could I have been a bit more accepting? Yes, yes, perhaps, I could have. You'll know, you'll see.

"Homecoming and Roots"
She took me to a house, made so cozily into a home. My home. It spoke to me, welcomed me with such excitement. My heart skipped a beat when I saw the painting made on my bedroom wall- "Happy girls are the prettiest." What a lovely memory! I vividly remember making it with my elder sister. Oh, so you ask about

my sister? She is the living embodiment of happiness; happiness in every pursuit of her life has been her biggest goal. She is a model living sometimes in New York or sometimes in Paris. You might think: a model and happy? They do sound like oxymorons but it's not true about her. That's why I admire her the most.

The bookcase was still standing tall in the corner of my bedroom. Dirty, yes but tall. I didn't learn how to write on my own. I discovered it accidentally. Funny, right? It was when I was fourteen that I found my passion because my long-lost friend cajoled me into writing a piece. I was surprised enough to know that it came naturally to me. It was my first poem: "*A Little Longer.*" Since then, I have made it into my escape; writing allows me to express another version of me that I conceal from the world and sometimes, myself too.

All this while, she stood patiently, lovingly, and wholeheartedly, at the door. I wanted to ask her name but it slipped my mind. Her calm vibes came towards me like soothing waves. It was clashing with the ricochet of memories.

After roaming here and there, and finding some old pictures, I decided to leave. Just at that moment, she started moving. Coincidence, it seemed.

The streets were green and the zephyr was playing with my hair. Things had changed so much but I felt stagnant. Around me, there were buses, cars, auto-rickshaws moving in a zig-zag and the shops were overflowing with diverse people. During those by-gone days, there were hardly any people on the streets. Just children playing and screaming with joy in their squeaky voices. I wanted that back because there was enough noise in my mind for it to physically manifest into my reality.

On my right, there were grocery shops. Yes, they were the harbours of my childlike cravings: of chips, chocolates and more importantly fun. My sister and I always went there in the after-school hours before my mum came home from her clinic. Sadly, the same grocery shop wasn't there, replaced by a big supermarket but I still stood at its entrance. Breathing in, I thought there might still be some remains of the old shop. Breathing out, I wondered - how could things change in such an abominably painful way?

I felt robbed of my precious memory.

"Teleporting"

I traced her footsteps and it felt like she was purposefully teleporting me to places that my heart longed for. It was time for my grandparents' house. It had always been my most loved place, located symmetrically between the beach and mountains.

I climbed the stairs and with every step, I could feel my heart racing a little faster than before. I was nervous. Shrugging it off, I went inside and my world caved in. I felt the sensation of pins and needles with every movement.

DPS GREATER FARIDABAD

From the corner of my eyes, I saw my grandparents sitting on the sofa, chatting, and relaxing. My maternal and paternal grandparents live together, does seem odd, doesn't it? They live in the most unique arrangement, to keep each other company at all times. The best part is that they were friends when they were kids. It's exciting how life can turn out like this!

They go about their lives, doing mundane chores, going to bazaars, and temples, in their traditional and peaceful ways. They have their close-knit community surrounding them at all times. They used to tell me how they lived through so much change and violence through the partition years. Their stories wreathed love, resilience, and most of all hope.

That place was my favourite only because of them. They took me and my sister to the beach whenever we went to visit them, showering their only granddaughters with so much love. I see it now, the love. They gave us anything we asked for and protected us from our parents' occasional scolding.

From the window, I saw her coming up, with her hair flying with enthusiasm and heard her sweet innocent shrieks of laughter. When she came in, she had already made herself comfortable. All of them started giggling and hugged each other so tight. Wow, that was sheer love. I felt sad to have outgrown them because of the time and distance. What could I possibly do to win them back?

Before going to college, I sat on the roof of this house, stargazing under the canopy of huge coconut trees, when I saw a shooting star. I made a wish and it did come true. No, it wasn't like a *fairy-tale*. It came with a collateral. I missed out on so many memories, while I was in Prague. It made me realize all the things I wanted back. On the roof, I found a place away from everything. The height made sense to me. I forgot all the pains of growing up, metamorphosing into a young adult with so many responsibilities, expectations, and tough feelings. Wait a minute, I am not too old, barely twenty-two next summer.

"Myriad Epiphanies"
My mum and dad now live in a farmhouse, away from the hustle and bustle of city life. I am not particularly fond of farmhouses, because I like the high-rise apartments and the thrill that comes with it. The adrenaline rush during teenage years fuelled me to rebel along with loud music blaring through headphones. But now I crave contentment, just like them. They were right. As always. I understand my parents better now, I see them for who they are. It just makes me love them more. Their perfect image is now juxtaposed with one that is raw, for they are both.

I didn't have an evergreen group of friends. Superficially, I talked to everyone but I just had one best friend during my good old days: my mother. My world started and ended with her. Whenever I had a bad day, both of us would go for a stroll at the central park, eat cotton candy, fryums, lollies, candies, ice creams, play with the dogs, buy toys, click pictures, go to the planetarium, museums, bookshops, temples, and local markets. She was my one and only source of happiness. I see it now, it's because of her childhood stories that I have become who I am today. I wonder if I knew her when she was young, would I be the same with her? Would I still be her best friend?

In the background, she was running behind the birds, and hens, while singing songs. What a joy, to be so carefree, alive, and truly happy! How much I miss that time! I wished to live it again just so I could appreciate it fully and not take it for granted. How would life be if we could turn back time? Maybe, it would lose its meaning!

"Strokes of life"
From my parents' farmhouse, I followed her to my school.

She held on to the gates of my school, and put her tiny head between its gaps. I used to do that too.

DPS GREATER FARIDABAD

It was here that I developed the valour to pursue my dream. Earlier, I was a bashful girl, very scared of every little thing. Going into dark rooms was my worst nightmare. Sounds so cringy now, doesn't it? But I have grown to be a fearlessly independent woman with the wildest of dreams and passions and aspirations. There's just no limit to what my mind can conceive.

My last year of school life was the most enchanting one. During that single year, I became exposed to another side of the world, one that was precarious but strengthening. My history teacher once said, *"You own your canvases, but how you paint them, depends on the mettle you show during difficult situations. It is easy to paint one stroke, but painting hundreds with the same finesse, it's called life."* It is still engrained deep into my constitution. I embodied every little lesson I learnt from my teachers, by observing them so closely. It helped me a lot during my vulnerable college years.

If there's one thing that I would want to do

YARN – WEAVING WORDS

Illustrated by Saara Gaur

again, that would be to tell my teachers how much I loved and respected them, and to tell them that they have touched and shaped so many young lives than most people can in a lifetime. It still wasn't late, though now, to tell them.

"Re-narration at the Crossroads"
She took me to the place where it all began; the place where I spent my last day in India. I was sitting on the river bank, facing the ivory river. I remember it was 14th December when I decided to go abroad, for the better. It had always been my dream since I was ten, to live outside India, graduate with the toughest degree and start my own company. I liked to be my own boss, and learn everything on my own, autodidact, I called myself. Throughout my childhood and teenage years, all I did was study and work. I liked what I did, so it wasn't a burden. But somewhere, I forgot how to truly live my life carefree.

I got lost in my thoughts again, as always, because that was the easiest. At that moment, she turned back and I saw her clearly for the first time. Her bangs swept across her dreamy eyes, and she looked exquisite under the periwinkle moonlight. She started walking towards me as I stood there, immobile from shock. Automatically, salt streams ran out of my eyes and I realized I had been following my younger-self the entire time.

She came nearer and I fell on my knees as she cupped my face in her little hands and wiped my tears. Guiding me through the re-narration of my childhood, indeed it was her. That's why she knew everything I liked and the places I wished to see or maybe I was seeing some hallucinations! Who would trust their mind in such a state?

Then, she whispered into my ears, whilst I hugged her tight, *"I love you and you have always been perfect. You grew up but you forgot where you came from. You battled the challenges all alone and you became so cruel to yourself, that you forgot how to be kind. You built the life you loved, only to wake up with a void of love for yourself. You forgot how beautiful your childhood was, and so many things were lost in the translation of your adulthood.*

You looked at me with angry eyes, thinking that I could have done better and tried to change yourself for the world. You need to know that I worked hard for you just so you can be who you are today and I did my best. There were many times when I was scared but I didn't give up on you... Right now, you exist as a mere being and I couldn't let my older-self suffer, so I had to take you on this solo-trip with me before you left again, to help you honour your sacred journey, to help you see your childhood through the jewels in your eyes and to help you live again. ... My darling, you are a perfect being, living an imperfect but beautiful life. Don't let your adulthood take your joy away. Remember, I am you and you are me. We're inseparable."

I had no words. But she knew how proud I was of her and how sorry I felt to not have loved her enough. My dad always said that ever since I was little, I had been a very mature girl, with a lot of wisdom. Ha-ha! I don't need any proof now!

YARN – WEAVING WORDS

Slowly, she let go of me. I asked her to wait a little longer but she insisted I had to let go of her. I didn't want to, anyway, who likes letting go of people?

There was no one around near the crossroads and it started becoming cold. I wrapped my arms around myself and whispered underneath my breath, "*I love you too*" as she walked away. I looked up at the purple sky and saw a Taurus constellation. Everything does happen at the perfect time, it seems.

While leaving, she looked at me and waved. All I could see was the silhouette of her body against the darkness. I waved back at her too, one last time.

"Becoming"

I opened my eyes to see that I had arrived in Czechia. My flight back was a journey to remember and most of all, cherish. After all the formalities at the airport, I reached my dorm room. When I opened its door, I knew I wasn't the same *anymore.*

NOT THE END.

DPS GREATER FARIDABAD

Life- A Hill of Ups and Downs
Author: Pakhi Gupta

Pakhi Gupta is a 13-year-old studying in 9th grade at Delhi Public School, Greater Faridabad. She takes keen interest in reading fiction and murder mysteries. Besides writing, she also enjoys dancing, baking and swimming. She aspires to be a successful entrepreneur in the future.

YARN – WEAVING WORDS

Life- A Hill of Ups and Downs
Illustrator: Rishit Mittal

Rishit is a 15-year-old student of class IX from Delhi Public School Greater Faridabad. He spends most of his free time sketching and creating new illustrations. He loves reading books as they help him think creatively. He is a perfectionist who works on minute details to bring his art alive.

DPS GREATER FARIDABAD

Life- A Hill of Ups and Downs
By Pakhi Gupta

What is life without the ups and down in it? A heartbeat is a wave that goes up and down when a person is alive. But when a person dies, the line is straight- no ups or downs. A life is only lived when there are ups and downs, like hills and valleys.

There I was on the couch in my pjs with chips in one hand and my ginger ale in the other, looking at Emma Verena on the television- the most successful business woman in the world. She was my biggest role model. I idolized her. I even wanted to be her.

But who am I? I am nothing but a naive 20-year-old named Sky Hansley, who has no idea what she is doing in life. I attempted being a gymnast, dancer, singer, and artist. I failed miserably at every single one of them. But then I saw Emma on the television delivering a powerful speech on empowerment and that is when I fell in love with the idea of starting my own

YARN – WEAVING WORDS

Illustrated by Rishit Mittal

business. Ever since, my dream has been to open a clothing brand. I would name it "Cotor".

I studied business and engineering at UCLA, but now I am just stuck with these degrees and nothing to do with them. I have dreams but that's what they are. I have no motivation to do anything in life. My personal life has been a little- well, you could call it messed up. My parents have always had a testy relationship and used to fight constantly.

Just a few months ago they filed for a divorce. Though I understood it was what was best for them, but after their divorce I felt like giving up on life. I felt like nothing was worth putting in the effort for anymore.

One foggy dull morning, when my meeting with the New York Bank for a business loan failed to impress them enough to approve my loan, I felt annoyed at myself and decided to take a stroll around the beautiful city of New York to clear my head.

YARN – WEAVING WORDS

As I was walking, a man who seemed to be homeless came up to me and asked for money. "Oh, kind lady, I have not eaten for two days and I have no money to buy food. Would you be kind enough to assist me?"

I decided to give the poor man the bagel I had bought for my lunch. He was so grateful when I gave him my meal that I ignored the fact that I hadn't eaten anything since last night. In an attempt to make a polite conversation, he asked me where I worked. This question has always irked me as it keeps on reiterating my failed attempts to make my life.

Somehow, this question from this homeless mendicant did not irk me as I compared my plight to his. It took me a minute to reply to his question, but when I did, I told him that I did not have a job, but I wanted to start a fashion company. He listened intently to every word I said and asked me why I hadn't started anything. Unwillingly though, I told him how hopeless I felt, something I hadn't even shared with my own conscious self. As I explained my desperation, I also felt a strange urge to talk to this mister nobody sitting in front of me. I had tried and I had failed, so what did that say about me as a person? Despair and hesitance were the only constants in my daily life.

The man shook his head. "Failure is a step in the path to success, my dear. It is not *life* that matters, but the *courage* you bring to it. Those who do not dare to try? *They* are the real fools," he said. Those were the exact words that hit me. It lit a sort of spark of clarity in me. Like a fire of passion; a wave of motivation. I was a bit startled that a man who was homeless, with no food, no money, gave me the courage to not give up, but I wonder why he himself did not bring courage to do something in life.

Why was he homeless? Why did he not have the courage to do something? Why did he not follow his own inspiration?

When I snapped back and wanted to ask him all this, I realized, he disappeared into thin air. He was nowhere to be seen.

YARN – WEAVING WORDS

I was confused by this man's mystery, but I also had a rush of motivation. Maybe it was the fact that a random stranger gave me courage. Maybe I knew it all along, I just needed to hear these exact words.

The next day, I woke up in the morning with a rush of excitement and a sense of responsibility, knowing that I held the power to change my life. It seemed that now, the tables of Sky Hansley's life had started to turn.

Now, the only thing I'd be quitting was quitting itself.

I enthusiastically began making plans on how to start the business. I finally came to a viable agreement with the bank, and took out a loan to start, which helped me buy a small shop in the Chelsey market. I put a small light up sign that read "Cotor", my brand name. Seeing that gave me hope, the hope to never give up. I had some designs drawn out and I started to stitch some of them. I worked all day and all night for months, sketching out designs after designs, again and again. As tiring as it was, I did not give up. The man's words gave me strength.

I finally came up with a few designs and I put up my designs to sell. I had been a month I did not sell one outfit. I felt like giving up. Maybe this is not meant for me.

But then I recalled the homeless man's words. *"It's not life that matters but the courage you bring to it."* I kept saying this sentence over and over till I regained back my courage. I cannot give up. Not now.

In five months I had sold out my first ten dresses. It took a while but I was all worth when I received the fruit of my labor. From that day onwards, I never looked back. For the first few months, I used to stitch all the clothes, but then the business started to expand, people knew my name. I decided to hire a few people to help me with the work, and the business kept growing. There was no looking back now.

YARN – WEAVING WORDS

In not more than two years, I shifted my headquarters to
Times Square. Yes, the unachievable Times Square. Many people end up just dreaming but I spent two years and innumerable hours to achieve this unattainable feat. I saw my brand name- "Cotor" on the front board. That is when I realized that all my dreams were coming to life. A few years ago, I was at the lowest point in my life. And now here I was, standing as CEO of a very successful company.

Skip forward to a year later, my brand was a household name. "Cotor" was a household name. *I* was a household name. I was now Sky Hansley- "One of the most famous fashion designers in the world." I got to do interviews, come on TV, cameras followed me, people asked for my autograph. It all felt like a dream, as if one day I would wake up and it would all end. But with every up there is always a down; that is the *mantra* of life.

Just when I thought life was all daisies and sunshine- "The business is in shambles. We are suffering *huge* losses. Not to mention, sales have reduced by 20%. And if this keeps going, we might have to shut down," exclaimed my manager, Emily. I could not believe what I had just heard. It was like my entire world fell apart. It looked like the news had spread. The second I stepped outside the headquarters, cameras and journalists were everywhere, and I was bombarded with questions.

"Ms. Hansley, what do you have to say about the huge losses your company has been suffering?"
"How did the company all of a sudden sustain losses?"
"Do you have any plans to save the company?"
"Are you planning to shut down the company?"

Shut down the company...? What was happening? I cannot shut down the company, no, never. But has it really come to this point, that I might have to shut down. All those questions were getting to my head. I felt dizzy. The world was spinning. I quickly got in my car and told my driver to drive as fast as he could. I just needed to disappear from the public eye for a while.

So, I did what I have always done when I needed to clear my head. I went to take a walk in the city (Undercover, of course) When I was walking, I saw the beggar again. One would imagine I had forgotten him; it had been a year. But how could I forget the one person who helped me get past my lowest point? I was so grateful to him, and I still remembered his words, tucking them away in my heart for when the going got tough. He was the one who gave me hope, hope that life was not over yet, that there was so much the world had to offer; I just had to go out and get it.
I went to the man with a bagel to give to him.

When I strolled over, he recognized me easily without giving it a second thought. He somehow was able to tell that I was sad and told me to sit next to him. "Everything is falling apart", I said with teary eyes. He looked at me and just said one thing, "It's not life that matters but the courage you bring to it". This line holds great power-the power to change a person, their destiny.

He stood up and walked away leaving me with more questions than answers. Questions about his identity, his wisdom, and his contrasting plight. His words ringing in my ears, made my questions about him irrelevant, as I had found my answers. It did not matter who he was or what was it that led him to this life. What mattered was, what he said. Listening to it gave me the strength I needed.

I knew I could not just give up now, after everything I had achieved. I started at the lowest point in my life, and yet I still could achieve success. I could still turn the tables. I could not give up my company, my dream. I worked day and night to bring this company to where it was. I cannot just shut down. A rose is beautiful, majestic, but it has thorns. That is what life is.

Leaving the mystery of the man behind, I

YARN – WEAVING WORDS

got into my car and went straight to headquarters. I told my manager that quitting was not an option. We all had worked so hard. We could not just give up.

I told everyone to gather in the meeting hall. I went up on the podium and took the mic.

"I started "Cotor" at a point in my life where I felt I could do nothing. But this company was, is and will always be my heart and soul. I have worked hard to bring it to where it is. We all have worked hard. We sketched designs over and over, stitched and stitched till late at night because this was our dream. We did not give up even when it got tough. We stuck together even during the difficult times. A part of me resides in this place. Every business has losses, that does not mean they quit.

In a heartbeat, a living life is shown by ups and downs. A dead life is a straight line, no ups, and no downs. We have had major ups in this company. Now this is our down. We have to handle it and fight through it with courage. After all, it's not life that matters but the courage you bring to it."

I do not know where all this came from, but it was what needed to be said.

Every single person in the room was teary eyed and started clapping. I took and deep breath and said, "This is just the start of a new era for this company. So, let's come together and bring this company to number one," I said as a true leader. I felt hopeful, as if the sky was the limit.

We started making new designs for my new fashion line. We took months just sketching designs. It got stressful at times but we did not give up. But I knew it would all be worth the struggle. We made roughly 50 designs. In another six months, we launched the line. People seemed to love the new designs and we were sold out of the first batch in a week. It was like my first designs all over again. All you need is a sprinkle of courage and the world is yours to conquer. There is no time like the

present to turn the tables over. Sky Hansley was back in business and there was no stopping her. I walked out of my headquarters, yet again bombarded by cameras. But this time it was different.
"Ms. Hansley, how did you do this?

"How did you literally resurrect the company?"

I was internally grinning. I got into my car and decided to drive to the place the poor man used to stay. I saw him and got out of my car with a bagel again to thank him. I decided to repay him for all he had done for me.

"You know, I never caught your name."
"It's Mark."
"Well Mark, you are very knowledgeable and you have helped me a lot. I want to repay you."
"Dear, it was all you. There is no need to repay."
"But I insist. I want to offer you a job in my company."
"God bless you angel."

I bought him a house and gave him work at my company as my assistant. Turns out he was very talented. I did always wonder what had happened in his life? He told me to bring courage in life but why did he not do that for himself? What went wrong?

I never asked him. I did not need to know. Maybe it was his destiny, maybe his choice. But you know what, whatever happened in his past went by. But the future is looking great for this man. Knowing the truth about his plight then seemed too insignificant now

If it wasn't for him, I would still be on my couch with chips in one hand and ginger ale in the other, watching Emma Verena on the television, wishing, and dreaming and not daring to try.

There is no right time to change things besides the present. I changed things in my life at a very difficult time. I didn't even know what to do with my life when I became one of the most successful businesswomen of the time. I felt like nothing was worth trying anymore. But just a few words from a stranger changed my entire life.

"It's not life that matters but the courage you bring to it."

DPS GREATER FARIDABAD

The Ghostly Nightmares
Author: Preeyam Das

Preeyam, student of class IX, is an avid reader who loves reading books of any kind whether it is fiction, or non-fiction. He aspires to be an engineer and his hobbies include cycling, reading and writing. Maths, Science and Computer Science fascinate him. Preeyam is tech-savvy and loves to explore new kinds of technologies.

The Ghostly Nightmares
Illustrator: Arpita Patel

Arpita is a 16-year-old easy-going person and likes to cherish every moment of her life. She loves creating new characters and weaving fictional stories in her recreational time as she believes that art is a way to refresh the mind. She has a pleasing personality and aims to become a Graphic Designer one day.

DPS GREATER FARIDABAD

The Ghostly Nightmares
By Preeyam Das

As Kevin was lying there on the floor of his house with his life flashing before his eyes, he heard a voice call out to him, it was his father. He said "You can do it; I believe in you". Kevin with all his strength left, managed to grab a fallen knife but then a sudden thought struck him, how did we get here?

30th May, 2035, the first day of his 11th Grade when schools had finally opened, 2 years after the T-33 virus pandemic which led to a total lockdown and online schools. Everyone, even teachers, were excited and looking forward to meeting their colleagues, but for Kevin, it seemed just another day at school when he met his friends Jerome, Robin and Martin in the school corridor.

Kevin's past was like a road covered with mist and fog. His paternal grandparents were from Germany who had seen the downfall of Nazi Germany as children. Not much is known except that they were murdered, by a killer who was long chased by the police but could not be found. However, he found a stick figure like wooden doll at his grandparents' house which Kevin kept with him as their precious memory. His father was a priest who died during the pandemic due to the virus and Kevin stayed with his mother Alice.

As the bell rang, Kevin took his seat in the class only to notice, a new girl had joined the class. Sasha, as she introduced herself to the class seemed very shy. As class started, everyone was amazed by Kevin's smartness. He answered all questions correctly. The lessons seemed to go by in a jiffy, then came recess.

Kevin was talking to Jerome about how dreams transport you to a whole new world, when he remembered the previous night, he had had a crazy dream. "I found myself in a haunted mansion. There were cobwebs in the house. Some sculptures were covered with white sheets… each one coated with a thick layer of dust. A pungent smell seemed to float around in the atmosphere. The flooring creaked on every step.

While exploring the place, I felt that someone was stalking me. Someone that wasn't supposed to be there... but still was. Watching, waiting. I caught a glimpse of a shadow a few times but never saw it completely. Little did I know what lay ahead for me" ....

Kevin continued "As I reached the bedroom in the house, I was shocked because of what I saw....it was a photo frame of my grandparents. That is when I realized that the house belonged to my grandparents and I bent down to see a Totem with eerie symbols and the word engraved "Rache" beneath their bed.

What was "Rache"? What was going on? I did not know but as soon as I got up, I spotted a monstrous demon with no limbs and a figure with a shade darker than black and eyes that looked like the moon clouded by fog.

I woke up at that moment breathing heavily and found myself in a pool of my own sweat. I turned on the lights and took a peek at the clock only to notice the time was 3 a.m...

Jerome interrupted "What did you think after you woke up?" Kevin replied "Was any of it real? Did it have something to do with my father? What was the figure? A million questions engulfed my mind, and with no answers; I was bothered. Well, I was not a toddler anymore that I could go and sleep with my parents so I slept again with the lights on."

Martin, who had just reached the group coming from the cafeteria; had overheard half of the story and took them to the computer lab. He was an expert in these "ghostly" matters and asked Kevin to describe the totem. What they found next was a horrifying coincidence. The engravings which this totem displayed made it clear that it belonged to a Satanic cult and 3 a.m. is when ghosts are thought to be the most powerful.

Robin who had followed the group now left saying "Oh C'mon! be rational, Ghosts don't exist, they are made up to scare children". An argument broke out between Martin and Robin, debating if ghosts were real or not.

Meanwhile Kevin decided to investigate the matter on his own. Not much happened after lunch, just an assembly on Environment. But Kevin's mind was still roaming elsewhere, thinking about the dream, the engravings and his grandparent's connection to it all.

The next day, as seats were changed, Kevin found himself to be a bench-partner with the new girl, Sasha. In an attempt to initiate a conversation with her , he asked her about her background; Where had she come from? What were her hobbies? What followed was the most interesting conversation Kevin had ever had which

YARN – WEAVING WORDS

Illustrated by Arpita Patel

included a diverse of topics like music, snacks, games, places etc.

During the sports period, all the girls including Sasha invited the boys for a girls vs boys volleyball match. Turned out, the coordination of the girls' team was on another level!

But the boys weren't going to back down that easily. However mid-match, Kevin started feeling sick. The wide playground looked like a creepy graveyard to him. The sun turned into a red-moon. There seemed to be vicious figures rising out from the ground however they were scared of him because of his father's cross locket. Then he saw a cursed ball-like object coming at him and he fainted...

When he woke up, the teacher asked one simple yet baffling question "What happened?". After hearing Kevin's side of the story, The doctor called it an episode of hallucination and said that he needed rest. After asking his friends how he had behaved, he figured the environment

YARN – WEAVING WORDS

around him had changed only for him and the cursed object he saw at the end was nothing but the volleyball. But like the one he saw before; it had a mark on it and symbols engraved
' ~을 위한'..

The questions "What were the symbols? What was its meaning?" bothered him but the nights were rather peaceful for Kevin after this incident. To lighten his mood, Kevin's friends and Sasha, who had become his best friend now planned a movie trip with Kevin.

The first weekend of the Semester sure felt wild as Kevin and his gang enjoyed in the mall. Robin, as always created a mess while choosing seats. Martin spilled Coke on the floor (which he got away with without anyone noticing). Sasha, Jerome and Kevin enjoyed taking tons of selfies and pictures in the background.

As everyone left, Kevin and Sasha took one comfortable walk in the park with the cold winds, the beautiful night-sky studded with stars and had a nice chat. Lastly, they called it a day and finally went home for a good night...... (Not for Kevin though).

He entered the dream world again to find that his father was fending off evil spirits in the forest when he stepped on a peculiar looking rock and fell down a never-ending ravine with no end in sight. The rock had a sign and the symbols engraved "無限大". Kevin however tucked hard onto his dad's locket and again found himself back in his room.

It was all crystal clear to him at this moment and he sensed the upcoming disaster....

He got Jerome and Martin on the phone who helped him decipher the engraved text. In under 15 mins, they figured out that the text was written in 3 different languages, German, Korean and Japanese. All the words combined together formed a sentence "Revenge for Infinity". The symbols which were also on the object were used by Evil demonic cults to summon demons.

The lights in his room went Fwooosshh and started flashing. The phone call went blank. There was just static Wrrrrrrrr noise from the phone when a voice with a pitch louder than speakers uttered the words 8th June and faded in an instant. Kevin knew the adults wouldn't believe him if he told them everything so the group started planning and called it "Operation Ghost".

The next day after school, the group consulted a priest about the symbols who agreed to tell them all about it on the condition that they would forget about it later and never see this stuff again. It was found that these 'totems', 'cursed objects' whatever you might call them, are used to curse someone and later a demon kills them.

There always had to be four victims for the curse to be successful and the only way to break it was 'Exorcise - the demon' which was practically impossible in most cases or you would have to kill the caster of the curse helping the demon. There would also be a number associated with this in special cases. Kevin was then convinced it was the demon and the caster who killed his father and grandparents and knew he had to stop them. The date was of some significance he figured but didn't know.

It was on the 7th, Tuesday, he had finally cracked the code.

The special number associated was 8. He said "Think about it. The date chosen was 8th. The ages of my father and grandparents were also multiples of 8.

Now all of us are 15 so it only makes sense the next victim won't be one of us. But as I see it, all the victims till now were from my family and my Mom's 40 now, so it may be her". Too big a secret to be kept now, Jerome went in and told everything to Kevin's mom who stood still in shock for a few minutes and finally moved to ask Kevin if it was all true and indeed it was.

YARN – WEAVING WORDS

She was alarmed so she called her husband's associates at the church to the house. And what a coincidence it was the same priest the boys spoke to the other day. The priest was an expert and quickly began to search the totem in the house.

Rooms were searched and to everyone's dismay, it lay right on Kevin's table, the stick figure like wooden doll which Kevin had found at his grandparents' house and had kept it with him was actually the Totem. The priest took the object and said he would help the family.

Kevin doubted himself since he didn't know a lot many things but as the sun went down on 8th June, everyone in the house was prepared. Prepared for a battle with none other than the ghost. It seemed like the silence before a storm when a knock was heard on the door.

The priest warned them not to open it, however it was too late.
Kevin saw Sasha at the door and opened it; however, to everyone's surprise, nothing

happened. Sasha just said "My birthday is on the 16th of June which is almost a week from today. I was wondering if you and your friends want to come hang out." Kevin wished a Happy 16th Birthday to her in advance and said he was busy in the middle of something so he had to go. Sasha shrugged at this confusingly and said "Yea I forgot to tell you people; I'm already 16 and going to turn 17.

Kevin had a revelation at that moment when he got the feeling of being hit by a lightning strike. He loved Sasha very much and Sasha was 16, multiple of 8. BOOM!

The door closed automatically and Sasha was thrown back to the ground outside the house as if the demon had done it. The lights and candles inside the house went out. Kevin tucked hard at the door and pushed open the door only to find Sasha being choked by the apparition.

He remembered his father's words "Pass this onto a person in need when you feel you will be safe" and put the locket around

YARN – WEAVING WORDS

Sasha's neck which calmed her down but the demon latched to him and tried to kill him by violently tossing him in the house.

Terrified at the sight of blood in the house, he looked up to see that the priest was indeed the curse caster himself and had pulled out a knife and injured his friends.

As his life was flashing before his eyes, he heard his dad's words of encouragement "You can do it, I believe in you" and grabbed a knife lying on the ground. He rushed right up to the Priest who was about to stab his mother, Kevin landed three hits, two on the leg and one on the hand to disarm him. The priest fell to the ground.

Kevin, thinking he had won and the storm had passed, dropped the knife and headed to hug his Mom when the priest got up and landed a fatal blow to Kevin. Kevin's mother did not care about anything at that moment and pushed the priest aside. Her rage was that of a mother who loved her son and killed the priest.

DPS GREATER FARIDABAD

The Police found the survivors of this incident and investigated the matter further. The pastor of the church stated that the curse was now completely broken and there weren't any ghosts but the demon was of German origin who had been killed by Kevin's Great-Grand-Father during World War 2 (Nazism) and the curse caster was a priest who turned to the dark side when he held a grudge against Kevin's Father which led him to cast the curse and call that specific ghost.

Kevin unfortunately could no longer survive and succumbed to the wounds and died....

Sasha and everyone's sadness couldn't be described in words but she promised to take care of Kevin's Mom. All of his friends survived too.

In the end, Kevin taught us the lesson that "It's not life that matters but the courage you bring to it" and gathered courage to do all the actions he did and protected everyone. It was his brilliance and courage that they could find the truth.

However, if we assume that the target of the curse was Kevin, then wasn't it successful? We may never know.

DPS GREATER FARIDABAD

All It Takes is A Drop of Courage
Author: Arnav Bhattacharya

Arnav Bhattacharya is a 14-year-old who loves reading books and writing them. He has many passions and aspires being an author. In his free time, he usually draws and sketches. He strongly believes in the quote that "a book is one's best friend."

YARN – WEAVING WORDS

All It Takes is A Drop of Courage
Illustrator: Devarsh Bhatia

Devarsh studies in class IX. He has diverse interests but his passion for books and art is profound. He can spend hours perfecting his drawings. He loves playing badminton. He favourite books are comics as they beautifully represent the stories through illustrations. He also loves reading novels written by Carl Sagan and JK Rowling.

All It Takes is A Drop of Courage
By Arnav Bhattacharya

A tall, lanky man was walking through a busy street. Finally, he reached his destination, a rundown house with its paint peeling off its walls. A few holes which were scattered on the wall, served as windows. The man went inside the house and removed his shoes. He was physically fit and had a handsome face with black eyes and black hair. He had a defined jawline and it was obvious that he worked as a labourer as evident from his well-defined muscles. Every child is given his/her parent's last name but, he didn't have one. His name was Rajeev.

He was an orphan who was hardworking and intelligent. He was quite poor but managed to make ends meet somehow. To everyone he seemed dull and uninteresting. But secretly he was inquisitive by nature. His dream job was to be a scientist but due to uncertain circumstances he wasn't able to become one as he could not pursue his studies after school to earn a living.

One day, as usual he went to work and as he was returning at noon, when someone stopped him. He was quite surprised as well as confused to find that the person was none other than his childhood friend, Karan, who was the only one in touch with him occasionally. "What are you doing here?" Rajeev asked. Karan laughed and said "Why, is it a crime to see one's friend? Anyway, I wanted to take you to our school's reunion party!" Rajeev readily agreed to go. They went to a restaurant where Rajeev saw all of his old school friends.

Seeing his friends after a very long time brought back a flood of memories. Just then one of his friends asked, "What are you doing these days Rajeev? I bet something big since you were quite bright back then!" Rajeev was somewhat embarrassed but told the truth anyway. After hearing he was just a worker, his friends started laughing and ridiculed him. Only Karan tried to defend him, but Rajeev was quite sad and so, excused himself from the restaurant and went back home.

On his way back, he found a newspaper on the road with an advertisement with a vacancy for the post of a scientist. For it, the applicants had to take an exam. He took the newspaper back home. At home, he was sure that it was a way of proving himself and so he began preparing himself for the exam.

It was just after another stretch of studying when a knock on the door startled him. 'Who might be at the door at this time?' he thought. He opened the door only to find a well-dressed man who was wearing a black suit which seemed quite costly. His eyes were covered with black glasses and he seemed quite unfriendly. The man also had a bunch of papers in his hand. He lowered his glasses and said, "Is this Mr. Rajeev?" Rajeev nodded in affirmative. The man smirked and said "You are being evicted from this apartment because of the dues that you haven't paid. We had sent you notices earlier but did not receive any response from you. Please clear the apartment by tomorrow. Thank you and have a good day." And he went away.

Rajeev was quite shocked as he had not received any notice. He was hopeful as he had some money in his bank account. Next morning as he reached his workplace, he was informed that the company had closed operations and did not need any workers anymore. He eased himself, thinking he still had some money in his account to pull through.

Rajeev wanted to withdraw some money from his bank account, so he headed towards the bank. There he, gave the details of his account to the manager present there and said "I'd like to withdraw Rs. 10,000 from my account." The manager looked baffled and said "But there is only a thousand rupees in this account." Perplexed, Rajeev asked the manager to look at the recent transactions. It seemed that a few days ago, someone had taken a lot of money from his account. That's when

Rajeev realized that he had accidentally clicked on a suspicious link a few days before. Perhaps that led to his bank account getting compromised. Rajeev told the manager that he had been scammed of his money. The manager then said, "In that case, you can get your money back but it will take about three months or so as we have to file the report."

Rajeev knew that his exams were in two months and till that time, he would have to survive somehow. Still depressed, he went back home (which was going to be his ex-home soon, he thought bitterly.) He packed most of his important things and books. He had no choice but to register himself in a rundown guest house for the day.

He was now determined more than ever to ace his exam.

No matter what the circumstances, he studied with a strong sense of purpose. The date of the exam finally arrived and he was all set. When he came out of the

YARN – WEAVING WORDS

Illustrated by Devarsh Bhatia

examination hall, he was sure he had done quite well. He was really excited about the results. After the exam, he came to the guest house where he had been staying for the past few days.

When he went back, the owner of the guest house demanded the rent for staying there. Rajeev found just enough money to pay for the rent but did not know how he would be able to manage in future as he had run out of money. So, he was forced to ask his friend Karan for help. Karan, upon hearing the difficulties of his friend, readily agreed to lend a helping hand to Rajeev with a smile. As a result, Rajeev was provided shelter and food, and he was rather grateful.

This went on for a week or so and after that, the results of the exam were finally declared. He reached the bulletin board where the results were.

He started from the last number which was 500. From over 30 lakh people, only 500 were selected. He skipped a few numbers but still didn't see his name. He was quite anxious by now.

He had reached the top 10 by now, top 5 now but still did not find his name. He saw the 2nd position but didn't see his name there.

His heart dropped and he looked away from the board, dejected. He still built-up courage and looked back towards the board. With this finger shaking, he slid it across the 10th position to the 1st one. There he was, the 1st position. He had scored the highest marks.

A lone tear trickled down his cheek but he still didn't do anything. After sometime he shook himself and realized, he had done it! He had cracked the most difficult exam and all it took was some courage.

The weeks after that went in a blur. He worked hard and kept learning new things and kept on working part time. He had finally become what he desired to be, a scientist! The cherry on top of the cake was that he got his money back that had been scammed off him.

A few years later, he was now one of the most famous scientists with many patents and innovations. His books on scientific discoveries were the best sellers and his theory on Artificial Intelligence in Robots won him a Noble Prize nomination that year and had also received a Nobel Prize for his discoveries and innovations.

He still remembered the time when he was poor and was on the streets. Now, he was one of the richest men and sat in a heated and comfortable office. All his so-called friends now started begging for forgiveness, and so he forgave them, even though he knew who his actual friend was. It was Karan who helped him with those hardships.

My father now closed the book and said, "Aryan did you understand the story?" I nodded and said, "Dad, the Rajeev person was you, wasn't it?" My father smiled and said, "That's a mystery for another day, remember it is not that life that matters, but the courage we bring to it."

He closed the door and went to his room where he called his best friend, Karan to inform him of getting a Nobel Prize. Now, I am sure that the character Rajeev, was indeed my father. I kept thinking about it until I fell into a blissful
sleep.

DPS GREATER FARIDABAD

The Nostalgic Smile
Author: Prisha Koshal

A young teenager in class IX, Prisha can usually be found reading a book and that will more likely be a realistic-fictional read. When not absorbed in the latest gripping page turner, she loves travelling, dancing, and learning new languages.

YARN – WEAVING WORDS

The Nostalgic Smile
Illustrator: Devarsh Bhatia

Devarsh studies in class IX. He has diverse interests but his passion for books and art is profound. He can spend hours perfecting his drawings. He loves playing badminton. He favourite books are comics as they beautifully represent the stories through illustrations. He also loves reading novels written by Carl Sagan and JK Rowling.

DPS GREATER FARIDABAD

The Nostalgic Smile
By Prisha Koshal

"Reshma, come here and help me in the kitchen!", said her Amma as she was sitting on the wooden maple coloured floor. The tantalizing aroma of hot steamed *idlis* and scrumptious sambhar wafted to her room and she couldn't stop herself from being drawn over to the kitchen. She hurried into the kitchen and the delicacies prepared had her drooling over them. "Wow! Amma has prepared so many dishes", she thought to herself. She spread the banana leaves and served the breakfast.

Born in a small village of Rasipuram, Tamil Nadu, Reshma was fortunate enough to be a resident of the village which was nothing less than a paradise. The purple hem of the sunset, the sweet enchanting notes sung by the birds, the beautiful variety of flowers all brought a sweet smile on her face. Reshma believed in simplicity. That day, she wore a white kurta embroidered with beautiful

YARN – WEAVING WORDS

patterns and black leggings. She tied her hair in a braid and tucked a small jasmine flower in it. Then she looked at herself in the mirror. She was all set to begin her day.

She then went outside and climbed up the mango tree that grew near her house. The mango tree brought back her childhood memories. When she was ten years old, she had built a small treehouse and this place became her spot of reading. Every day, she would climb up the tree, escape from the everyday household tasks and read a book.

That beautiful morning, her dusky skin gleamed under the sunshine and her brown eyes sparkled with excitement. She grabbed a book and started reading it. Suddenly, her gaze fell upon the beggars sleeping on the grey pavements and women carrying pots of water across long distances which could be seen from high above the tree. Acknowledging this reality of some of the people in her otherwise beautiful village, a tiny wish to become a civil servant, crept into her mind and her resolve to help the downtrodden sections of the society made her determined to achieve her goal. Suddenly she heard her Amma calling her in a scared voice. She came down the tree and hurried into the house. And the news was indeed heart wrenching.

Reshma's family lived in a rented house. That day, the owner had sent a letter stating that he wanted them to vacate the place for he was coming to stay there. Poor Reshma and her family members were panic stricken. Although, they knew that they could not spend their lifetime in that house since it was a rented accommodation yet finding a new place to reside at such a short notice was difficult. The very thought of parting from her tree house had made Reshma really sad. Just then the doorbell rang.

"Who could it be?" Reshma thought to herself as she went to open the door. She was greeted by one of their neighbours.

YARN – WEAVING WORDS

He said, "It is so sad that you are leaving this village. It would be a pleasure for us if you stay at our home. "The family made up their mind to accept the offer as it would give them some time to look for a good rented accommodation. They decided not to trouble their neighbours by staying at their place for too long. However, to make the matters worse, Reshma's father lost his job. So after having stayed at their neighbour's place for about two weeks, they bade them goodbye and went over to her Patti's (grandmother's) place who lived in a village in Kunnam.

A month had passed by and witnessing this tough situation of her family, Reshma was sad and pensive. Nobody had been able to comfort Reshma. Her parents were way too busy dealing with the financial crisis the family had run into. They had not even noticed that all the current events had taken a toll on her mind. Reshma did not know what to do to help her parents. If she told her parents that she wanted to go to Delhi to pursue her studies, she would come across as too self-centered. She did not know with whom she could share her feelings. She did not have anyone to confide in and so, she decided to write her feelings. She started making a note of everything that she witnessed and recorded her emotions in a small pocket-sized diary.

Days passed by. Indian festivities of Thaipusam filled the village with happiness and joy. Children sprang up in laughter while the women of the village were preparing sweets to offer to goddess Parvati at the temple. That day, to commemorate the occasion of Goddess Parvati giving Lord Murugan a vel, Reshma's Amma and Patti paid a visit to the Shri Kailasanathar Temple. They offered milk, water, fruits and flowers to the deity. After the puja was over, they seated themselves at the bench and talked of how they could contribute to the family's income during these tough times. They decided to use their passion as their profession and started selling homemade pickles. This did help them a bit

YARN – WEAVING WORDS

Illustrated by Devarsh Bhatia

improving their financial condition.

One fine day, Reshma was asked to fetch water from the village well. Her Patti went in her room to make the bed when her gaze fell upon a small pocket-sized diary. She realized that it was Reshma's. As she flipped through the pages, she had a shock in store for her. She realized what Reshma was going through. She did not want to share this with Reshma's parents for the news might trouble them. She decided to help Reshma by talking to her. When Reshma came back home after fetching water from the well, she was called by her Patti. She asked Reshma to get dressed up and accompany her to the nearby Azheekal Beach.

They walked out of the house towards the beach. It was evening. Tall coconut trees made the pathway dark. As they walked, they could hear the splash-splash of the waves. Reshma and her Patti sat down on the sand and enjoyed the wet salty sand's fragrance which made the environment even more balmy, serene and tranquil.

YARN – WEAVING WORDS

After some time, her Patti narrated her a story of her childhood. "You know Reshma when I was a teenager, I was going through the same mental trauma. Once when I was walking by the beach side, I had a chance meeting with Arun, a talented painter who was making a beautiful painting on the canvas sitting on a wheelchair. I was intrigued to know more about him. He told me that he was an athlete but due to a car accident in his early 30s, his legs had to be amputated owing to which his life changed completely. It was as if he had slept in one world and woken up in another.

Instead of letting that depress him, he fought back and continued with his passion of painting. Later, he even opened up his own painting school and today he teaches the skill of painting to thousands of young students. He taught me that it is the way you react to adversity and not the challenge or adversity itself which determines how the story of one's life will develop.

Reshma, I want you to inculcate the same values in yourself and not lose hope."

That day, her Patti's words kept resonating in her mind and she kept remembering them. Even during the night, she wanted to hug her Patti for giving her hope and positivity to surge ahead in life. She tiptoed into her Patti's room and hugged her tightly. She came back to her room and slept peacefully.

The next day she informed her parents of her plans to study for UPSC exam. Determined to achieve her aim, she burnt the mid-night oil to prepare for her exams. Her Patti was happy that her words had an impact on her. After having worked hard, she gave her first attempt. She was hopeful that she would clear the exam. By then her family's financial situation had improved. Her father had found a job in a small firm and they were hopeful of a better future. On the day of the result, Reshma was overwhelmed with excitement. In the morning, she prayed to God and then opened her laptop. She entered her roll number on the official website but there was a shock in store for her. She failed to clear the exam. She felt so disheartened that her days were filled with sadness and tears.

Suddenly, she remembered her Patti's words," It is the way you react to adversity and not the challenge or adversity itself which determines how the story of one's life will unfold." She decided to give the second attempt and this time worked harder. Her heart was beating faster than ever and she was trembling before her result. She was over the moon when she realized that she had cleared the exam! Her dream had come true.

Soon, she became the District Magistrate and everyone was proud of her. She decided to write a book on her life's story. The book titled, "Your Attitude to Life's Challenges" became the best seller. As she held the book and read the title, a sweet smile crept on her face,

DPS GREATER FARIDABAD

The Power Over Destiny
Author: Garima Singh Chauhan

A student of class IX, Garima Singh Chauhan is an avid reader and an aspiring author. She loves reading horror. Other than writing short stories, public speaking is one of her other talents, as she has competed in various events. She aspires to release a full-length novel one day.

YARN – WEAVING WORDS

The Power Over Destiny
Illustrator: Arpita Patel

Arpita is a 16-year-old easy-going person and likes to cherish every moment of her life. She loves creating new characters and weaving fictional stories in her recreational time as she believes that art is a way to refresh the mind. She has a pleasing personality and aims to become a Graphic Designer one day.

The Power Over Destiny
By Garima Chauhan

"Madam saheb? They're ready for you now..."
"I'm coming Bahadur"

The reporter entered the lavish room, guided by the sharp-looking assistant. He looked around. The room was dark beige with only light oakwood furniture. The soft fragrance of chamomile flowed freely in the atmosphere. The assistant excused himself for a second to call upon the "star" of the day —-- The famous 60-year-old activist, Ameerah Rizwan. She was known both in her days and by the current generation. She stood up for the citizens' rights, protected innocent people and voiced their opinions.

And most importantly, she helped the refugees in various refugee camps in India, during the partition of India and Pakistan. Today was the day she was to speak about her life story. She had been awarded the prestigious Padma Shri award, and now it

YARN – WEAVING WORDS

was time for the press conference. He was the first reporter to finally speak to her after the ceremonial obligations. His company had given him the privilege of doing so.

"Ma'am, it's a great honour to meet you finally.", he said, standing up, as she walked into the room. Her frame was frail and small But that did not stop her from exuding confidence when she stepped in. A daring smile and a pep in her step told the reporter, this might just be worth the pain of working overtime.

"Good to meet you too beta. I hope I can make your time worthwhile with this story of mine. I thought it is time I should finally share with the world what constantly motivated me to help as many people as I can."

Her voice was low... but did not go unheard. The room full of cameramen, sound managers and light managers went quiet for a moment just to hear her speak. "So, Madam Ameerah Rizwan, shall we start the interview? The first question I would like to ask, and the nation would like to know... what is your story? What helped you keep a clear mind during such chaos, that you helped over one million refugees find peace after the dreadful partition of India and Pakistan? You stood up for people before that, and assisted in letting the general public recognize basic rights."

Nervousness and peace, two contradictory emotions pooled in the bottom of his stomach as she started her story. He couldn't help but look excited, a glow on his face.

"It all started back in 1937... I was exactly 18 at the time. India was a country crowded by foreign powers. The country had been occupied by the Mughals, the Portuguese, the Dutch and then finally, the residing power... The British. They were not more than traders when they came, but as time flew, the Britishers expanded their territory and power. And finally took over the country, home to a variety of people and kingdoms. All bound under one rule.

YARN – WEAVING WORDS

My Ammi, Abbu and I lived near Lahore. At that time, the country was undivided. The city in those times was not as modern and reformed as it is now. Half the streets and most of the buildings were close to demolition. But that didn't stop most of the citizens from living a decent life.

My Abbu was a farmer, and my Ammi was a housewife. Both jobs did not affect our safety, for we had no connections with the activists or protestors. Most of our relatives were based in Central Delhi. My Ammi was of Hindu origins, so every time lives were lost, she would go and pray for a longer time. Praying for our safety, praying for our country's safety. I would watch her do so and sometimes, even join. I still remember the year, 1931.

I was exactly 12 at the time, a kid really. But that didn't stop me from trying to understand exactly why my Ammi was concerned about the safety of our country. The famous revolutionary, Bhagat Singh had been hanged that day. She chanted her prayers as usual. But I could see the melancholy look on her face... tears rolling down. When I asked her about it, she could barely respond.

Anyways, we lived in a small colony full of farmers and workers like ourselves. Most of the families were just like us. Trying to make ends meet and feed their families. The colony was completely dependent on a farm that most of the people shared, for profit. The Britishers had not yet touched this part thus, we were quite safe. Everyone would earn a decent amount of money, enough to survive.

Most parents wouldn't dare to send their daughters to school. But my Abbu was extremely different. He wanted me to receive proper education, and someday, help the country attain independence. His dream was not to see me play a huge role, but even a small part in the ongoing revolution would do. Contribute my patriotism and energy to the movement. The revolution to drive away the Britishers from our country.

YARN – WEAVING WORDS

Illustrated by Arpita Patel

I remember the day to this date, a changing point in my life. The day I found out exactly why I wanted to fight, not just for the freedom of India, but for the basic dignity of the citizens. 24th of November 1937. The sun was shining through the clouds. As I was walking back home, I noticed smoke rising from the colony. I rushed to see exactly what was happening.

The sole source of income for every community member, the field, was lit on fire. Every single crop, every piece of hard work, being burnt to ash. Nothing was left. I couldn't believe my eyes. I still remember the very sight of it. All of the villagers were gathered with buckets of water, trying to douse the flames. My Abbu and Ammi were there too. I watched frozen for a split second, then finally regained my senses and ran to help everyone.

When I questioned my parents later in the day, it turned out that the field had been burnt by a band of rowdy teenagers protesting against the Muslims in the locality. The idea of a different country for

YARN – WEAVING WORDS

Muslims was quite vague at the moment, but apparently, enough for some people to destroy the property of innocent people. They had not planned for it to go this wrong, but it did. And now, we the villagers were the ones paying the price. It was British India, it was not like we could collectively go to the government, or a police station just to complain against them.

I felt horrible. My parents and I would probably have to shift and find a new settlement to continue with our lives. We couldn't possibly live here anymore. No one knows what other heinous acts the people might pull. And the worst part was that we couldn't do anything to stop it. We were just a middle-class family... trying to survive in the revolution-ridden India.

We soon moved to another village. My dad found the same occupation, working in the fields, day and night... trying to earn us some money. I was already grown enough, so my Ammi started to suggest the idea of marriage. While my Abbu was against the idea, once my Ammi was determined for something to happen, neither of us could possibly change her mind. Soon enough, Abbu gave in to her pleas to marry me off. Just to keep me safe from any possible harm by being part of the revolution. Little did they know, participating in the revolution would not cause harm, rather this marriage would.

I wanted to study further, harder. Achieve something for myself. Maybe even help India attain freedom. But at the time, it all seemed like a goal I couldn't quite reach. I soon got married to one of my cousin brothers who had to shift to Lahore to find work. I couldn't possibly find another groom, because our family was far too poor to fulfil the needs. The marriage was reclusive, with only some old colony members and friends attending as a mere obligation.

My husband was a cruel man. He always abused me. Beat me up, and I couldn't do anything to protest because I would be letting my parents down. I soon learned to live with whatever violence was inflicted upon me."

Ameerah had tears in her eyes. Her voice was breaking down, but she didn't stop. The blaze in her eyes was still there, just this time, it was shining brighter than ever. As if reminiscing the incidents which empowered her to go on. She continued...

"The scars of the battles I fought long before I started protesting are etched deep in both my mind and body. Never fading, never-ending. I couldn't take the constant abuse anymore. One day, I finally made my decision. To run away. I packed my bags, took out whatever money I could save, away from my husband and I boarded a train to Central Delhi, hoping to find some allies amid all the chaos.

Soon enough I found refuge among some other immigrants, workers and activists. We all shared a small room in an apartment. Protests would take place every day, the crowd getting more and more agitated. I decided to try and fulfil my father's lifelong dream for me. To help India gain independence. For 10 years, I took part in any possible, small or large protest in the city. I refused to fear the Britishers. What was happening was wrong... people couldn't complain to anyone about what was happening in their lives because none of us were sure if our cries would be heard, or silenced like million others.

The only thing that I regret is leaving my Ammi and Abbu behind. I gave no notice of the fact that I had escaped from my failed marriage but they were probably worried about me. No will in me could go back to what could happen back home. They had wed me off. They wouldn't think twice before doing it again. Marriage was the only future for a woman then.

Then came the year 1947. I had been hearing the news of the partition for quite a long time, but little did any of us know that it would happen. The partition of India and Pakistan. I couldn't believe that when the Britishers finally decided to leave the country, they decided to divide the whole country in half. But I had vowed to myself that I would become part of the bigger movement. I wanted to help people find peace in the chaos. While the states most affected were Punjab and Bengal. I operated from Delhi. Helped a million refugees board trains, and find shelter. Protect themselves. Get themselves to safety.

In the midst of it all, I received a letter from an unknown person. I cannot explain in words the pitfall in my stomach that I experienced the moment I read the letter. It was from a doctor in Lahore.

My Ammi was on her deathbed. An incurable case of pneumonia. She had been suffering for the past 3 months, and not once had I paid notice to any of her letters or my father's. Burned them in the furnace without a second thought in an attempt to part with my painful past. When I got there, she was already looking weak. Her skin was a sickly yellow. A local doctor was tending to her.

"Ammi... I am so very sorry I didn't visit you often. I didn't know you fell this sick. I was part of the revolution in Delhi. I ran away Ammi, I fulfilled Abbu's dream."

"Ameerah beta, I'm aware of what you were doing, and believe me, I don't regret not meeting you very often. Because your work is noble. Your Abbu isn't here to see your progress... For he passed away long before. But I know in my heart, he must be very proud watching you from heaven. It was his biggest dream that you help the masses."

"Abbu...
When did it happen? How did he..? Did the Britishers get to him? What was it? Why isn't he here... Why isn't he alive!!"

I bombarded my poor mother with questions. But the news of my father's death was something I wasn't quite ready to digest. I had achieved what I had aspired to be on... but on the path to this platform, I left behind my parents. I left behind the people who raised me. And I wasn't quite ready to accept the fact that I did so.

"Beta… your father got caught up in one of the riots happening around the local train station. He wanted to board a train to try and find you. To convince you to come back home after receiving no reply in return of our letters. But… the riots did not stop. The rage I felt against the Britishers was unimaginable. My father was a peaceful man who had conducted no harm to any person in his life. None!! And still just because he wanted to come to see me, he died. He died because of me… The guilt of this incident haunts me to date. "Ammi… I'm so scared. I don't know what to do anymore. Abbu died because he wanted to come to see me. I feel scared Ammi… what do I do?"

The next thing that she said is something I remember to this date. These words I can never forget…

"Beta, it is not life that matters… but the courage that you bring to it. You must not

be afraid. Be strong, be brave. Make your Abbu and me proud. Whenever you feel like quitting, remember how far you have come. Your father never wanted to stop you. He wanted you to be part of the revolution going on in India. And now you are. Don't lose hope Ameerah. For your Abbu's sake.
Khuda Hafez beta... may Allah be with you"

Even in the coming days, when the government of India was still fragile, I helped people realize their potential. Harness the fear and rage into power. Power to change our destiny. We are Indians, and we do not have to be subjected to foreign rule to sustain ourselves. This was my story. My story as to how I came to help millions of people."

As she spoke the last word, the camera stopped rolling and every single person in the room started clapping. The reporter himself couldn't believe that he was not just talking to Ameerah Rizwan an activist, but also a daughter, a woman and an

YARN – WEAVING WORDS

Indian. And somehow, her identity was only defined by her actions.

That's how big her actions were. She commanded respect for a reason, and the reason was that she stood up for herself, for her nation. Even after a so many hardships, she did not give up. She rose even stronger. And that was the pinnacle of success only a few could achieve.

Fight For Justice
Author: Kriti Bansal

Kriti is a class IX student who loves to pen stories in her free time. She is a nature enthusiast and loves to go on long walks or a cycle ride. She likes exploring the creative side in her whenever She strongly believes that on must keep on learning as there is always scope for improvement.

YARN – WEAVING WORDS

Fight For Justice
Illustrator: Sehar Yadav

Sehar is 14 years old studying in IX class. She has a panache for drawing and loves creating sketches. She aspires to be an entrepreneur. She also enjoys reading books and writing

Fight For Justice
By Kriti Bansal

A city within a city *Dharavi*, infamous as one of the world's largest slums was home to Ajinkya. As dusk set in, Ajinkya was one among the many from his slum who thronged to the *Abhyas Galli* to study under the halogen lights which unlike others did not attract bugs that troubled studying children. Lined by tall trees on both sides, this quiet place with bright lights, clean benches was a haven for students like him as it offered him long nights of undisturbed studying away from his small abode made of tin sheets and scrap metal.

He lost his mother when he was just nine and lived with his father who was a daily wage worker. The very thought that his mother could have been saved only if proper treatment was provided to her still haunted him however making him more and more determined to fulfil his ambition of becoming a doctor, so that he could give people correct treatment on time and save lives. Ajinkya was a bright student and his teachers at the local school encouraged him a lot to pursue his goal. Next day when he was coming back from school, Ramu Kaka, his father's cousin who lived nearby, informed him that his father had met with an accident at the construction site. "We have to go see your father Ajinkya! He has got hurt." said Ramu Kaka in a tone that startled the boy. Both hurried to the site to see his father.

He was severely injured and thus, in a lot of pain. The contractor on-site reported it and called an ambulance. They did not want to get into any trouble so they made sure he was taken to the ER as soon as possible. Ramu got in with his father and ordered Ajinkya to go back home.

Feeling helpless and scared, he did not want to go back. Before he could enquire about how his father met with an accident, he heard some of his father's co-workers talking amongst themselves. "This was bound to happen! These rich businessmen don't care about our lives. All they care about is their profits. If only they had installed a net and better safety equipment, Ajinkya's father wouldn't have fallen and hurt himself..." A silent rage grew within him against the people as their negligence caused his father's suffering.

Within a few weeks, his father recovered and returned from the hospital. The cost of the treatment was borne by the owner of the firm he worked in but they refused to hire him back as the nerves in his right arm had been permanently damaged and he wouldn't be able to work. Ajinkya and his uncle went to get his father from the hospital.

He told Ajinkya, "*Bade sahib* will soon fire me and since I am not capable of work anymore, so we wouldn't have a means of livelihood. I know about your goals, son. But you will have to quit school and start earning for both of us." The mere thought of dropping out of school made Ajinkya shiver. He told his father that he needed some time to take such an important decision and so he began contemplating his options. He used his uncle's phone to

YARN – WEAVING WORDS

Illustrated by Sehar Yadav

find out about his father's situation and found out that his father had been wronged by the firm. According to his research, it could not fire his father because he had been injured due to its fault. It had not been taking appropriate safety precautions. A great many labourers had been victims of the same treatment by "Aadekar and Co.", the construction company.

Ajinkya's Dad was losing patience waiting for his son to make up his mind. This made Ajinkya scared of his father forcing him to leave school. It was all that he could think of day and night.

One sunny day, while coming back from the medical shop which was in the bigger city (out of Dharavi), he felt blinded by a huge board that reflected the sun's rays directly at his face where he was standing. "R.K Husain and Advocates (Specialization- Corporate and Criminal cases)"

It took some time for him to read it with the sun flashing in his eyes and it could have also been his exhaustion of walking since so long but there was a twinkle in them when he got the idea that filing a case against his father's firm would get him the justice that he knew his father deserved! He tried to enter the office but seeing his shabby clothes and worn out *chappals*, they denied him entry and told him to go away. The boy became very upset. He decided to try to reach the lawyer every day. So, every day he would stand outside the office requesting the security to let him in, but to no avail.

Rahman, who was one of the lawyers of that firm noticed him waiting in front of his workspace. In the evening when he was returning home, he saw that the child was still there. He was astonished to see him and felt bad for the child. Out of curiosity he said, "What are you doing here young man? You should be at your home studying or getting ready for bed!" Ajinkya replied, "I need your help to get my father justice. Please help me, Sir! The guard did not let me go inside and I could not talk to you so I waited for you to come out." Rahman's heart melted. He too had a tough childhood in poverty. Rahman decided to help Ajinkya. But as it was getting late, he told the little boy to come to the office at 9:00 am the next day. His father's case would be the first thing he would look at the next morning.

The following day, Ajinkya arrived sharp at 9 am in the morning. Rahman was impressed by his discipline. He understood that this case was important for the boy. Rahman realized that that was the case for him too. Though all lawyers are supposed to keep their personal interests out of the way while working, he couldn't help but feel a connection with Ajinkya. He decided to do his first pro bono case in a while. Ajinkya was waiting at the door when Rahman came and took him inside with him. This time the guards could do nothing. After reaching his cabin, he asked Ajinkya- "So what happened to your father?" while pulling out a chair for the boy to sit on.

Ajinkya replied in a hurried and bothered manner, "My father got hurt while doing work because the rich people didn't pay heed to his safety! Now he cannot work because of his right arm and I will have to quit school to make a living. I want to study sir, please help me!" Rahman was touched. "What about other adults in your family? Can't they earn? "he asked. Ajinkya told him that his mother died when he was young and there was no one except his father's cousin Ramu who was not financially sound either. "Hmm, I can help you. But, only on one condition..." Ajinkya got worried as he had nothing to give to the man.

Their savings had been depleting due to the costly medicines. Rahman chuckled "Oh don't get so upset! I don't want money from you. I just want you to promise me to study well once I help you get your father justice." Ajinkya's smile returned and he agreed happily. Listening to the enthusiasm in his voice, Rahman got an inkling that the boy was interested in studying more. It reminded him of himself as a child and his desire to become successful. "Bring your Ramu kaka to my office tomorrow at the same time and we'll discuss the case," said

the advocate.
Ajinkya went directly to Ramu kaka's house to convince him to meet Rahman. who was cross with Ajinkya for going behind his father and uncle's back to talk to a lawyer. "You shouldn't get involved in all this *beta*! We don't have the power to fight big businessmen no matter which lawyer you go to. Apart from that, we cannot afford Rahman as a lawyer. He is well-known and must be expensive." Ajinkya told him that Rahman was doing it for free. "Are you sure Ajinkya? You are not getting spammed by someone acting as Rahman sahib, are you?" Next morning Ajinkya took Ramu kaka to Rahman to clear his doubts. A bit hesitant to file a case against his former boss at first, Ajinkya's father also joined them and visited the office. Suresh, Ajinkya's father told Rahman each detail of the case and also brought in a very helpful witness.

On the day of the trial, "Suresh Gaonkar versus Aadekar and Co.", everybody was nervous except Rahman. It was his unique trait to stay calm in the most stressful situations. He knew that the man he was representing was a victim and wanted to get him justice. When Rahman disclosed to the judge that appropriate safety measures were not taken, the owner of the firm denied outright. He said, "My lord, that is completely false. We care about our workers very much and would never do so!" Rahman called a worker who formerly worked at the firm and testified against the businessman. He had left his job on the day of the accident as he was afraid that he could have the same fate. The verdict was given in favour of Ajinkya's father and the businessman was told to give a hefty amount as fine. He also had to by starting the use of safety precautions and give all injured workers a part of their salary every month. Everyone was elated as justice had been served.

Ajinkya kept his promise. He studied earnestly and worked part time so that he could afford his education. He became an accomplished doctor and helped the poor by providing them medicines for free. He served the meaning of his name very well as it meant 'The Invincible'.

A Navy SEAL's Mission Account
Author: Anubhav Dash

Anubhav Dash is in class XI. He is passionate about penning gritty crime fiction. Raymond Chandler, Dan Brown, and Sidney Sheldon are just a few of the authors he enjoys reading. When he isn't creating stories, he loves to assist children with special needs in collaboration with Prabhat NGO.

YARN – WEAVING WORDS

A Navy SEAL's Mission Account
Illustrator: Yashvardhan Singh

Yashvardhan is a class XI student. He is passionate about sketching and bringing alive the characters of stories and illustrating the connotative meaning of poems. The world is his canvas and he loves to sketch his perception of things around him.

DPS GREATER FARIDABAD

A Navy SEAL's Mission Account
By Anubhav Dash

Part 1: Suspense

It was 2:18 am. We were in a Boeing Chinook, waiting for further instructions. The cabin of the helicopter was dark, chilly, and lit only by a few tiny red overhead lights that allowed us to see one another. After making a brief radio contact with the USS Nevada control towers, we anxiously awaited for the go-ahead to takeoff.

As the chopper lifted itself from the deck of the enormous ship, I felt my heartbeat quicken. The chopper cabin was filled with a palpable sense of tension and suspense. I could see Major Thomas attempting to project calmness in front of the boys. I tried to fall asleep, closing my eyes and dreaming about my wife, Anne, and how we had first met in Colorado's Sebastian Garden. But instead of hugging me, she bolted and dove into Loch Rosaria. Oddly enough, she shouted out for assistance as she sank to the bottom of the Loch. Even though I could hear her screams, I was unable to act to save her because I was

YARN – WEAVING WORDS

paralyzed with fear. I was groggy when I abruptly awoke. Although it was a nightmare, the cold, green water that was rushing all around me was real.

The alarms were blaring. Everyone was cursing while attempting to protect themselves and their fellow soldiers. I observed Major stumbling as he attempted to assist me in the surging waters. I firmly grasped his hand as he extended it to me. Then my head received a severe blow from something. I started to lose my vision. While unconscious, I was able to feel the chilly water that had reached my chest and realized that we were in the frigid, shark-infested Mediterranean Sea without any moonlight to light the sea.

Part 2: At Home
Wednesday
September 19, 2017
9:14 pm
Dear Diary,
Well, the good times are once again over. After receiving a call from headquarters, I was instructed to return to the closest

airbase with a code. I have to be there tomorrow morning at four. And who knows my 10-year-old daughter Jeanne better than you? She begged me to quit the Navy so I could spend more time with her, sobbing uncontrollably as she reminded me of the commitment, I had made to her last October. Although I had no immediate plans to leave the Navy, I did my best to comfort her. After comforting her, I finally finished packing my bags and got her to go to bed, but not before giving her one last kiss on her cheek because she will be dozing off when I leave tomorrow early in the morning.
Good Night

Part 3: Seeking Ibrahim
On the USS Nevada, the whole SEAL Unit-4 was assembled. I took a C-17 Globemaster flight earlier in the day from the Nevada airfield to Beaumont, Texas. There might be a covert mission taking place underground since I went through a thorough inspection, which happened as if I was going to meet the president as a regular citizen. We were required to hand

over all our communication tools to a deckhand by the name Robin McLear even before we boarded the ship, USS Nevada.

I realized then that our masters had something significant in store for us. The bombshell was dropped on the night of November 7th, when we received a last-minute order to gather in the dining hall. Three soldiers in high-level uniforms sat in front of us on a stage, gravely discussing something, before Major Joshua Child, a former Marine counter-insurgency specialist with a distinguished military career, introduced himself. The second was Sergeant Major Tommy Hillson, a decorated veteran, and former naval SEAL. Captain John Murphy, a member of the SEAL team who had assassinated Osama bin Laden. He was quite an intriguing individual.

"Commandos, the next few words I speak will give you the chance to set your military record apart from others," Mr. Joshua said as he started the meeting. "Before I give you more information, remember you will not be able to contact anyone outside the mission until it is over. Everyone in this room is aware that Ibrahim Hassan has been killing American service members in Iraq with the assistance of various rebel organizations. However, we were able to locate him, when some CIA officers stationed there were successful in determining his whereabouts. They discovered that on December 11 in the Atlantic Ocean, around midnight, he would strike a weapons transaction with an underworld don, Mikey Hazel-wood. They also found the location coordinates where they would be meeting, the details of which will be shared with you all soon." Everyone had been listening intently, their mouths open in awe at the chance they had been given. We returned for the second briefing the following evening. "This will be our last briefing," Captain John Murphy said at the beginning of the meeting.

"SEAL units one and two will be under the leadership of Major Thomas and Major Rayson. Ibrahim Hassan from the MV will be eliminated by Major Thomas' team.

YARN – WEAVING WORDS

Illustrated by Yashvardhan Singh

DPS GREATER FARIDABAD

Mikey from the MV Endura will be eliminated by Major Rayson's team. Commandos Matthew and Johnson will jump into the sea to mine the MV Adonis and MV Endura's draughts and detonate them after all the SEALs have departed the vessels. By utilizing a hooked rope to ascend onto the stern of the vessels, both majors will lead their respective units onto the deck.

The units will then split up into five teams of four commandos each. All the terrorists on the deck will be eliminated by two teams. The aft hatch entrance will be used by the other six to board the ship and accomplish their objectives. It begins at one in the morning and you must accomplish your objectives and report back to the USS Nevada by four in the morning. You will be dropped 3 miles away from your targets by two Chinook helicopters. You will next use four rigid-hull inflatable boats to travel in the direction of your targets from there. Over and out."

YARN – WEAVING WORDS

After the briefing, we all went to our cabins. I entered my cabin and discovered a huge man standing there. I did not disturb him as I went to sleep in my bunk bed while observing him complete some paperwork on the table. He woke me up, apologized, introduced himself as Jimmy Weil, and asked for mine. After the introduction, he spoke about his family's journey to America after the Holocaust, his difficulties before joining the military, and his eventual enlistment in the SEALs. He paused and said good night after noticing that I was having trouble staying awake.

We started live-bullet training with other commandos the next morning. There, I learned that a man by the name of Roald Keenan would be my mission partner. We trained for almost 15 days on limited sleep and some physically exhausting activities. All the time, I was attempting to put Anne and Jeanne out of my mind so that I could concentrate on the task at hand. I walked out onto the deck every night to look at the starry night sky and tried to identify the constellations.

DPS GREATER FARIDABAD

Part 4: The Surgical Strike
Without any losses, we successfully climbed aboard the RHIB after escaping the sinking chopper. The other unit boarded their RHIB almost immediately after exiting the helicopter as the other Chinook hovered over us. We had been dropped at least seven miles away from our intended destinations, according to our compass. Surprisingly, it took us 19 minutes to cross the distance stealthily. When the two assigned SEALs arrived at the sites, they dove into the water to attach the explosives. A hooked rope was thrown onto the stern by Major Thomas. Onto the deck, everyone ascended. The two teams charged with clearing the deck then moved on to carry out their objectives as we boarded the ship using the aft hatch door.

Everyone ducked for shelter when a sudden fire burst and hit us. I hurried into the captain's cabin and saw him draw his weapon. I fired my M-4, as my conscience ordered me to do so. In three shots, he was gone. I left the room and went outside into the alley. Another round of shots was fired at us, and they did not appear to stop. Everyone instantly realized that we would all be dead if we did not act quickly. The firing abruptly halted. I anticipated the outcome. I leaped from my cover and hurled two grenades toward the terrorists who were in hiding. I was completely deafened by the grenade explosion. It appeared they would send everything wicked to hell. I curled up into a ball as I could feel the flames surrounding me. After the explosion, I began firing haphazardly in the direction of the terrorists' cover. All the commandos then emerged from hiding and assisted me in standing up. Even though I was feeling weak, I knew I could keep going because of my determination. At least nine to ten people, all of whom had been burned to death, were lying on the ground.

I looked around but could not find Roald. I informed Major, and accompanied by another commando, William Nelson, began to look for Roald. I heard whispered conversations as I searched for him, so I warned William to be careful in case the terrorists opened fire on us. We found the

DPS GREATER FARIDABAD

Conference Hall from where the whispers could be heard. Nelson and I took positions on either side of the door. I gave him the go-ahead to smash the door. He quickly entered the room breaking the door, and I quickly followed him. I hardly had time to comprehend before I fired at Jimmy.

The left side of his chest was pierced by the first shot. He was struck by the second round above the heart. He was struck by the third round above the eyebrow. The fourth his forehead and the fifth struck his left ear. Blood gushed from above his brow. He tripped over a table and raised his hand as he fell, perhaps saying his goodbye to me. I collected my thoughts and assessed the circumstances. Nelson was holding an AK-47, and Ibrahim was standing about two feet away from me with a Glock pointing at my head. He threatened to shoot us if we did not let him go. I glanced at William who understood what I meant and we both shot Ibrahim till we filled his body with the last bullet remaining in our magazine.
We assisted Roald in getting to his feet.

YARN – WEAVING WORDS

Jimmy was going to kill him if we had not intervened quickly. He revealed to us that Jimmy was Ibrahim's aide. He was a mole planted in the SEALs to give classified information to the terrorists in Iraq. Roald had spotted Jimmy guiding Ibrahim to safety, so he questioned him about it at gun point. Then Ibrahim struck Roald in the head, and Jimmy snatched away his weapon and was ready to kill him when we came just in time to save Roald.

When I radioed Major about this situation, he promised to arrive as soon as possible. When I heard gunfire in the back alley, we all proceeded covertly to eliminate any surviving terrorist. I quickly turned around the corner as I got close to it and fired blindly at the figure of a man who was standing at the opposite end. I sprinted in his direction and kept firing at his outline. I knew it was a SEAL as soon as I got to him and saw his slumped body on the ground. Major Thomas was on the other side of the body when I flipped it around. He was gasping for air and whispered something into my ears before taking a final deep breath, following which he did not answer any of my calls. Despite wanting to panic, I kept my composure. Nelson and Roald suddenly approached my side, peering at me horrified and distrustful. I told them that I shot the terrorist who was dead near Major and not Major himself.

We were instructed to immediately leave the vessels and head back to the RHIB. While others provided cover for us, we swiftly sealed Ibrahim's body and took him along with Major's body. Other SEALs instantly took control and assisted in carrying the bodies to the RHIB as we approached the stern. I felt something hit me below my neck as I was running away, and I was suddenly overcome with pain. Bullets sparked on the metal all around me and ricocheted as I leaped from the stern deck into the RHIB. I landed on the RHIB using my legs, which presumably lessened the impact of jumping from such a height. Other SEALs under the cover dragged me as they frantically struggled to cover the retreating commandos. Our ammunition was running out.

YARN – WEAVING WORDS

I could feel the RHIB being throttled at top speed before I witnessed a magnificent firework when the explosives were set off. The lack of the moonlight meant that the stars were shining brightly, magnificently illuminating the night sky. Although the pain was getting worse, I was feeling better. I could almost see my physical therapist saying that my fitness depended on how quickly I was able to recover. I fell unconscious.

Part 5: Flashback
It was Anne's birthday. We flew to Florida to celebrate her 34th birthday, leaving Jeanne, who had been two at the time, with her grandmother. We lodged at a hotel called Rio Venetia, which boasted a private marina. She insisted that we go on a yacht ride a day before we were supposed to depart. I assured her that I was fine and that she should ride a yacht while I relaxed at the marina with a cocktail. Since there were strong winds that day, she decided to ride a sailing yacht. But around noon, the wind blew so hard that her yacht capsized in water, and she, never a swimmer herself,

called out to me for help while she was drowning in water. When the staff heard her cries, they rushed to the marina. By the time I could reach, it was too late. It was so sudden that my numb mind could not comprehend the situation. I could only make out the overturned yacht and her floating body after the wind died down. Even though my parents and her family had forgiven me, I would never be able to explain to Jeanne why I was unable to save her mother or even forgive myself for the it. My parents wanted me to remarry so that I could take care of Jeanne, but I declined because I knew that only her lovely mother, who was now deceased, could provide Jeanne with the motherly love she deserved.

Part 6: Award Ceremony
"Major Mark Hemsworth is awarded the Medal of Honour for his "outstanding bravery and intrepidity above and beyond the call of duty" while saving the lives of 5 Navy SEAL operators on Mission Atlantis and for killing Ibrahim Hassan and his associates ..." The senior officers and the

men applauded as I approached the podium to get the Medal of Honor pinned on my reluctant chest. I smiled for the photographer after receiving the medal because I could now clearly hear Major Thomas's final words, "It is not the life that matters, but the courage you bring to it," repeating in my thoughts."

Part 7: Home Coming
I opened the door with tears in my eyes, feeling a wave of remorse wash over me. I removed my boots and snuck inside Jeanne's room. She leapt up on the bed when she saw me and gave me a hug akin to Anne's. I could no longer hold back my tears. This happened a very long time ago. I am no longer serving in the military on active duty. FBI investigation determined that I had shot a terrorist rather than Major, as I had initially believed. I am yet to come to terms with Anne's accident. And yes, I stare at the night sky every day and know every constellation and star visible in the night sky by heart. I light a candle every now and then in loving memory of Major and Anne —not very often though.

DPS GREATER FARIDABAD

Dared to Dream
Author: Anusha Sharma

Anusha has always loved the written word and regularly shares her views through school magazines and newspaper articles. She has also got the privilege to meet renowned authors like Ms. Paro Anand and Mr. Pragati Sureka who greatly inspire her. She agrees with Isaac Asimov's statement, "Writing, to me, is simply thinking through my fingers".

YARN – WEAVING WORDS

Dared to Dream
Illustrator: Devarsh Bhatia

Devarsh studies in class IX. He has diverse interests but his passion for books and art is profound. He can spend hours perfecting his drawings. He loves playing badminton. He favourite books are comics as they beautifully represent the stories through illustrations. He also loves reading novels written by Carl Sagan and JK Rowling.

DPS GREATER FARIDABAD

Dared to Dream
By Anusha Sharma

The night of 24th July 2004 was life changing for the 13-year-old, Yang. With a lean physique and an affable aura, Yang, unlike the other girls from her village, was very ambitious. She belonged to the Hmong caste which is found in many western countries even though it is considered unworthy in countries like Vietnam, but in China, it was accepted with pride.

The Hmong tend to be inclined towards sports and play many of the ethnic sports including Crossbow. The Hmong caste was one of the most colorful castes with beautiful and attractive attires and a variety of festivities. However, Hmong people strongly believed that women were inferior to men. The women of this caste were obligated to perform just the household chores and nurture the babies.

Yang had grown up reading Jane Austen and Louis May Alcott and though being surrounded by such people who were so

YARN – WEAVING WORDS

insular about women had developed a rebellious side towards people who had a biased and opinion towards girls and women.

Brought up in a penurious family, Yang had to face many troubles. She was deprived of many necessities which girls of her age took for granted. But from the beginning she had a fighter's attitude towards her problems. That night something was on her way which was tough to fight against. Did she remain that ambitious strong-headed Yang? Let's see...

The moon hid behind the clouds making the dark night darker. The street lights blinkered and her footsteps echoed on the streets as Yang headed towards a roadside store down the street to buy some medicines for her father who had been coughing restlessly due to his deteriorating lung infection. Suddenly a screech of a jeep trailed behind Yang. As the jeep stopped, four young men jumped out of the jeep, wearing black masks and had ropes in their hands. She knew the danger was lurking behind her and fastened her footsteps. She started to run but one of the men with a well-built body and a height nearly 5 foot 5 caught up with her. She struggled to get rid of him but to no avail. They tied her with the rope as she screamed "Help! Help!" They made her sit in a black jeep as it rushed into the dark street ahead. The strong blow of the wind felt as if it was screaming and letting the people know about the abduction of the young innocent Yang. But alas! Only if those blowing winds had words maybe Yang could have been saved.

Three days passed, Yang was kept in a room which carried nothing except a bench and a jug of water. A small slit at the door which allowed sunlight to pass through the room. Crying for help was all that Yang could do for the last three days. She would sit by the slit at night and would sing "Shishangzhiyou mama hao"("Only mother is good in the world"). She was missing her mother terribly, how her soft tenderly hands would brush Yang's dark brown hair as she would sleep in her mother's lap.

YARN – WEAVING WORDS

On the bright day of 27th, after three days of her captivity, in keeping up with the tradition of the Hmong people, she was declared the wife of her kidnapper. It was beyond her imagination that until yesterday she was just a young school-going teen and today she was someone's wife!

She screamed saying "No, I can't marry now. I am a young girl. I must achieve my dreams, my wishes. One night can't destroy my happiness! Please, I beg. Leave me, my parents would be worried about me." The man laughed, "Dreams? What dreams? Don't you know that your only purpose is to be a wife and a mother. And, forget your family now. You are married to me; my parents and I are your family."

With anger, frustration and disappointment reflecting in her moist eyes, Yang said boldly "I don't consider you, my husband. I don't agree with this marriage, and you can't go against my will. LEAVE ME!"

The stranger husband retorted domineeringly, "Your will? Don't you know about our tradition of Bangjia Xinniang? If a man wants to marry a girl, then he and his friends kidnap her." Having said this the man locked the door again and the room was filled with the sound of whimpers in the eerie silence.

It was a shame that such a tradition existed where kidnapping was rampant killing the dreams of young girls like her. Ah! She remembered how belonging to a village like Bachuang, it was quite natural for the police to not react to the pleas against the Bride Kidnapping. She remembered how once one of the ladies living in her neighborhood had gone to the police station to report a FIR against her drunkard husband who would beat her. But that poor lady herself got insulted by the station inspectors for getting the thought of imprisoning her husband. Afterall she was a 'woman.'

But Yang was determined about her dreams and aspirations to become a lawyer.

YARN – WEAVING WORDS

Illustrated by Devarsh Bhatia

She knew that her life could not stop because of a tradition that she did not believe in. She could not kill her dreams just like that. Yang was a girl of courage and determination. She was not like other girls who could bury their ambitions within themselves. She planned to free herself from this trap of abduction.

She knew that the slit in the door of her room was her way out to live up to her dreams and aspirations. Late at night when she made sure that no one was awake, she broke the glass jug and with the piece of the broken glass made the slit bigger and passed her hand through it to open the locked door. She ran from there until she was out of breath and sure that she was away from her tyrant abductor.

She thought of going back to her house and was confident of her parents' support. As she knocked the door frantically and on seeing her mother a sweet relief spread through her heart just like an ink drop spreads in the water. But it was exactly opposite to what she had hoped for. As she unfolded the events of past three days and revealed the truth of her absence, her parents abandoned her coldly as according to them she must return to where she was married. They declared that she was no more their responsibility. This shattered Yang and she felt betrayed by her parents. But she knew that she had to do something to make her dreams come alive.

From an early age, Yang had a strong belief on Goddess Nuwa, the Goddess of bravery and courage. She prayed to her Goddess and started planning for a fresh start. When you lose everything in life the only thing that makes you survive alone is hope.

She went to her friend, Jing's house wherein she found a shelter to live and some food to eat. Jing was Yang's classmate, she understood and supported Yang's decision. At a tender age of 6, Jing was left at her uncle's house by her single mother. Struggling with financial problems, her uncle too had to leave her in the lurch. So, from an early age Jing had been working in a restaurant to earn her

living. Yang decided to live with Jing and worked in that same restaurant to earn some money. In no time Yang started living a life of definite hardships but pure independence. She worked at evenings and did her schooling in the mornings.
Years passed by with flying pages of calendar. Yang had a strong determination to fight for all those girls like her
who had to face this absurd custom of Bride Kidnapping.

She knew that to give shape to her dream she had to become a successful lawyer. She decided to appear for the Law entrance exam. Yang worked extremely hard for her exams conducted by the National College of China where she could earn a scholarship as well. She had been burning the candle at both the ends.

Finally, the day arrived when she appeared for the exam. She did an exemplary job in the exam and got a wonderful rank with the opportunity to study in one of the best National Law College of China. She knew that she was close to achieving her aspirations and any work in haste could lead to her dreams slipping away from her. She completed her 4 years graduation from the Law School and finally became a lawyer who was ready to begin her law practice. All this while, Jing supported her wholeheartedly.

One fine day while walking down the street she saw a young girl with a begging bowl. It was usual to see such young children with begging bowls but this seemed a bit different to Yang. The girl had normal attire unlike the other beggars who had torn dresses and unruly appearance. She went to that girl and asked "Hey, why are you here with this begging bowl?" That girl replied "I have no home, no food, nothing! It all happened in just one night! That's why I am here, here with this begging bowl"

This intrigued Yang more about what exactly happened in one night that made a young girl sit with a begging bowl. She was another victim of Bride Kidnapping; she knew it was the time to avenge this ritual. She took Fang, that young beggar to her house fed her with a comfortable meal and asked her just one question, "Are you willing to fight against the men who kidnapped you and turned your life upside down". The pain in that girl's eye, the tremble in her voice when she asked "Will I get my home back?" made it clear to Yang what Fang had been through and she knew what she had to do now.

Yang registered a PIL against child marriage and coercion for a matrimonial alliance. She even tried to meet and talk to Fang's parents to win their trust and support. But they turned down Yang's request. She saw the same denial that she had seen in her parents. But she knew that it was not going to be easy and she had to win the case to win the faith of all such parents. The PIL got accepted and Chang who had kidnapped Fang was summoned to appear in the court. Chang was affluent and so he too put up a famous lawyer to fight for him. On the date of hearing both the parties met in front of the judge. The case began; Yang put up her charges and proved with a revolutionary tone while

YARN – WEAVING WORDS

Chang's lawyer was more defensive. Soon, the media covered the strong objection taken up by Yang and it was discovered how more than half the girls in the country had to give up their education and childhood for the sake of the custom and ended up serving their husbands unhappily.

With the clock ticking at 5pm in the evening, the verdict came and with a heavy voice the judge said "After making a lot of considerations we have reached the conclusion that under the Child Marriage Act 2006, and Article 240-241, we ban Bride Kidnapping. The court orders Chang to pay for Fang's education as a punishment." A sudden murmur spread across the courtroom just like the fire in the forest. But the murmur did not impact Yang.

She was lost in her thoughts remembering her sacrifices, her pain and her suffering. Yang grinned from ear to ear and was now after so many ears proud to prove the world that she had taken right decisions.

Can We Meet
Author: Parnika Pande

Parnika is a passionate teenager who enjoys reading books and writing poems as well as stories. Her stories reflect the characters with a delicate sense of mystery and intense emotions. Apart from her studies and hobbies, Parnika likes to contribute to help other and make the society a better place.

YARN – WEAVING WORDS

Can We Meet
Illustrator: Pratishtha Mohanty

Pratishtha is a seventeen-year-old. She has always loved to read, enjoys interacting with others to improve her writing, and is an intellectual who relishes learning something new every day.

DPS GREATER FARIDABAD

Can We Meet
By Parnika Pande

CH 1
Rukmani

I haven't taken a shower for three days. Nothing has been able to get me out of bed, one I've been told I am lucky to even have, since the hostel I live in can't pay well for the very purposes it is supposed to serve. My roommates don't bother to check up on me either. It's almost funny to imagine a scenario of them for once not taunting me throughout the day, constantly picking on my complexion not being as fair as theirs, taking advantage of my introversion and reticence, comparing my grades to theirs and the list goes on. It's not as dramatic as I'm making it seem, however. They're manipulators who bring you down in subtle ways.

I don't normally pity myself but on these rare occasions, I'm forced to introspect sitting in this dim room accompanied by overwhelming silence. I think about my parents and how they must be doing. Do they miss me? Do they think of contacting me? Do they talk about me amongst themselves? Do they regret throwing their sixteen-year-old daughter out of the house for not wanting to become a doctor and choosing Arts instead?

They had always been so rigid. They took my story books away by the age of 10 and replaced them with math and science ones. But they couldn't take away my imagination. I wrote poems, short stories and haikus most of the time and quickly hid them when they appeared around. Well, it was time to select my stream and for once in my life I decided to be bold. I went up to them, my chin up and back straight and told them, "Mom, dad, I know you've wanted me to pursue the medical field, but I know sincerely that this is not for me. I have neither the aptitude nor the interest."

My mom dropped the plate she had in her hand, or she threw it. I can't quite recall. My dad's eyes were filled with rage. They felt betrayal and confusion, which I thought was genuine until I knew it wasn't when my dad told me to get out. I couldn't believe what I had heard. They didn't *want* to understand me. What followed was an hour of shouting from both of them and my mom finally dragged me to the door and pushed me out of *their* house. Not ours any more. Now I was the one experiencing betrayal and confusion.

The next few months I lived with a close friend of mine. Her parents were generous enough to take care of my education for the next two years. I got into a good government college to major in English literature, the fees of which I could pay by myself by freelancing.

And now I'm here.
I rub my thumb over their photo on my phone as I realize I have been introspective for a little too long and each time this little crying session is of no use. No further perspective, no new explanation- the same old story and the same old me, still quiet, reserved, and shy.
I hear my roommates outside and pretend to go to sleep.

YARN – WEAVING WORDS

CH 2
Mr. Doshi

"I have so much love for you dearest. Where will I put it if you leave me?" I asked my ailing wife.

"Oh, you coward! Put it somewhere it'll stay forever. Books, words, phrases. You know, books never die." She said.

"Silly woman!" I snapped at her. "So quick to reply, as if you had already considered the possibility of leaving me! Go to sleep."

That was our last conversation.
She was referring to my lost love for my passion- literature, reading, writing, and teaching. When she was sick, I put aside everything and focussed on her. I stopped working, stopped reading books, stopped going to libraries and just sat at home taking care of her. She knew how much I loved what I did and thus wanted me to return to it. But after she died, I wept for months. It took a lot of courage to change myself, but after one year, I thought it best to follow her advice.

DPS GREATER FARIDABAD

Although I was a 65-year-old retired English professor, I still wanted to help struggling writers. I came across www.writersnet.com, which connected writers with professionals for improvement. It had been a year since I had set up my profile and received barely any requests until today from a nineteen-year-old Rukmani.

CH 3
Rukmani

I have had enough. I need to do something. I had put my soul into the book I've been writing. I don't understand where I have gone wrong. It got rejected again. I was thwarted yet again by those chauvinistic publishing houses.

I also have my exam sheet in my hand- 42/100. I am doing horrible. My life is spiraling again, not that it ever got better after leaving my parent's house.
It is evening. Meghna, one of my roommates, barges in, looking at my sheet, "Poor Rukmani! Honestly, if I were you, I would give up at this point." And she goes

into the washroom with such casual strides, it feels like she is genuinely unaware of how much that phrase could affect me. I begin to wonder if she is right. What if I had no talent to start with? What if my parents were right? And I'm too shy to talk to my professors to seek their help to become better.

I need validation from someone, from anyone. Just a few words assuring me I didn't make a mistake choosing this, that I still have it in me, that nothing is wrong with me.

I switch my phone on and type- "Sites to connect with writers and readers." The first platform that pops is www.writersnet.com. I quickly set up my profile and browse people who appear before me. They all look pretentious as if they are all doing it just for the money. I scroll down until I see the picture of an old man maybe in his 60-70s offering his help for free. He looks genuine. I click on "REQUEST" and send him the same book I had sent to the publishing agency. I write in the additional box asking him for feedback and start rambling about my current situation. I have to get it out of my system. So what if it is to a random older man I found on the internet?

I click "SEND" and fall to the bed, not wanting to think about how miserable all this feels.

CH 4

Mr. Doshi

I took 3 hours to read this girl's book- All chapters in one sitting. I'm still sitting in the same position on the chair. I am too amazed. I don't know who this girl is, yet I know so much about her through her little description of her life and the type of characters she put in her story. For her to think so less of herself stuns me even more. I have a lot to tell her.

I begin typing on my computer everything I should tell her- the good parts, the loopholes, why the houses are rejecting it, key points, and encourage her to be more outspoken. I empathize with her as well. While writing, I reflect on my life. How the passing away of a loved one made me lose my senses. How I felt like a coward- following the routine of sleeping and eating each day for an entire year. It took immense courage to lift myself off this pit.

I felt it was important for Rukmani to do the same, to lift herself too by being confident and bold, by showing her true mettle. So, I last write the phrase I think best suits her circumstances, *It's not life that matters but the courage you bring to it.* I hit "SEND".

As I get up from the chair, I feel a sharp jolt run through my chest. As if a heavy stone had hit it. The pain is excruciating. It doesn't stop. I feared this day would come. I didn't take my heart medications regularly. I shout for someone to come, but I live alone, my only son lives far away from me in a different state. He had abandoned me in a sense; he thought I was too much to handle. It's funny how in my last moments, I am thinking about Rukmani and how similar we were in strange ways.

CH 5
Rukmani

A *real* person wrote this? A *real* person thinks my book reflects great brilliance? It took me fifteen minutes to read everything Mr. Doshi wrote- and that's when I call myself a fast reader. It was a 13-page document detailing everything I needed to know. In the last two pages he talks about my personal life and his personal life. His words are so encouraging that I get tears in my eyes. I feel determined. I feel *new*.

I open my book without wasting a second and start inculcating his value points.

It's 8 in the evening and I realize I have been on this laptop for six hours. My fingers have given up. I save the changes and get up from the chair. All I need now is fresh air. I head downstairs and walk down the street.

Half an hour later, when I return and open the door to my room, I am met with an uncanny sight- All four of my roommates looking at each other and the laptop screen, perplexed. Their countenance changes when they see me.

"When will you write a real book Rukmani?" Asks Meghna.
"W-w-what do you mean?" I stammer, "That's the final draft."
They all gasp and I feel a sense of foreboding. "Final?" Exclaims Natasha, "This looks like a draft- the *first* draft. No wonder they rejected you twice already."
Reeva interrupts, "Looks like you're going for a hat-trick Rukmani." And they all start chuckling.

Tears well up in my eyes.
Meghna comes forward and says "Aw, look at you. We didn't mean to make you cry; we just wanted to be real with you; story writing isn't everyone's cup of tea."

And with that, they leave. I'm alone again in the same dim room with its painful silence. All the memories revitalize.

I fall to my knees and cry the hardest I have ever cried. I deserved to be thrown out. I deserved to be shouted at. I deserve to have social anxiety and no friends.

In the midst of this sadness, anger surges. Anger towards Mr. Doshi. I can't believe he would do such a thing to me. This is what I get for blindly trusting strangers on the internet. Or maybe he wasn't a real person after all. Just some bot typing random words.

What am I even saying? I need clarity. I need to know why he lied. I need to understand why he would give hope to an inept, useless, incompetent person like me. I start a war on the keyboard and write everything that comes to mind. I hit "SEND"

The last day of submission of my final book is three days from today. I was so sure of submitting it just an hour back. I go to the washroom and look at myself in the mirror- red cheeks, red nose, swollen eyes, scattered hair. I wash my face, tie my hair and come back.

YARN – WEAVING WORDS

Illustrated by Pratishtha Mohanty

My last glance of the day is the tab adjacent to the one opened on the laptop- Mr. Doshi's first mail to me.

CH 6
Mr. Doshi

A few people are mumbling and shuffling about. This does not feel like my bed, and the ceiling, as it slowly comes to focus, is not the usual white that I wake up to everyday. I try to open my eyes fully but there is a daze in my head, a tightness all over my body, stemming from my chest. I hoist myself up and lean on unfamiliar pillows. White coats everywhere. Wheelchairs whirring outside my room. An intense smell of floor cleaners. This is a hospital.

I try to look around and I see Mrs. Agarwal talking to the doctor. She must have brought me here. She is nodding vigorously, and as she leaves, the doctor approaches me on seeing that I am conscious. "You have survived a heart attack, Mr. Doshi. It is a miracle that you are awake right now, but you are at risk of another one if you do not take care of yourself. Believe me, I would be on alert if I were you. He has a curt manner of speaking, what a way to deliver bad news. Crisp and to the point, sudden like an attack on your life.

As the doctor hurries out of the room, I try to recall the moments before I ended up here, but everything is a blur except for my laptop screen. "The email!" I startle the nurse with my urgency. She diverts her attention from the water bottles on my side table onto me. "Can you take me home? Can someone take me home? I need my laptop; I need to reply to her!" She tries to get me to lean back, her voice is calm and strangely soothing. "You really need to relax, Mr. Doshi. I would not recommend getting so worked up right now. The doctor needs to keep you under observation still, so you cannot go home, but I can get your neighbour to bring your laptop here, if that is what you would like?"
"Yes, yes please." I say gratefully.

***

I am awash in thousands of different emotions after reading her email. As I compose a new email to her, my mind is buzzing with her words, that poor girl who does not even know that she has a gift. Wasted, unrecognized potential is the greatest tragedy, and it is a wonder how we move through our lives, doused in fear. How do we even do it? "I do not know what I am doing with myself, I do not know why I write every day, why I even think that I can achieve the status of a real author." She has written this and more in her email, a letter of pain.

I wish I could have her see what I see. My fingers are already tapping away on my keyboard as I try to take away her world of pain. I fill pages upon pages full of love and understanding, rightful appreciation and kind criticism. But most of all, I try to put into words how she must never, ever stop writing, how she must never think herself unworthy of achieving the ambitions she chose herself. Why do our own choices scare us? Why do we lock ourselves up?

YARN – WEAVING WORDS

Why is shame bigger than us? I do not have an answer to these questions.

But I do have the answer to one: Despite this all, what would we ever do without courage? The answer is, nothing.

I realize I have been typing for an hour and even then, there is so much to say, this is not the time to hit SEND yet. I reach for a drink of water before I resume but I feel a sharp, painful sensation in my chest. I try to lay down, but I am already breathless. It feels like all air is escaping out of windows and ducts, and all I have left is a vacuum to breathe in.

Even amidst all of this constriction, I remember that this is the feeling that carried me to this hospital. It is happening again. Where would I be carried to after this? Another hospital? Things become blurry. I hear the reverb of hurried footsteps, but all is slow in my mind. As the darkness carries me into another world, I hear the prolonged beep of the ECG machine. And then it all stops.

CH 7
Rukmani

It has been three days since Mr. Doshi has not replied to my mail. Is he angry with me? Does he think I don't deserve an answer? Maybe after what I wrote to him, he thinks he probably had it all wrong about me.

I read his first mail each night before sleeping. And I wondered each night, how he induces emotions in words so well and how he knows exactly which word at which place would strike the heart of the reader.

The one phrase that keeps echoing in my mind is -"*It's not life that matters, but the courage you bring to it.*" What I'm about to do in just thirty seconds feels exactly like the first time I did it.

With my chin up, and back straight, I stand in front of ASCENT PUBLISHING HOUSE. I go inside with a smile and hand the assistant my book.

***

I'm in my hostel room. It has been a week

since I gave my book in. I'm sitting in front of the laptop, with my inbox on the screen, still scrolling through it to find *maybe* I had missed an email from Mr. Doshi.

I sigh. I have been re-checking for days. I would have found it by now. I close my eyes and instantaneously hear the incoming mail sound. "Mr. Doshi!" I open my eyes and exclaim.
Oh. It is not from him.
It is from Ascent Publishing House.
It is from Ascent Publishing House.
My book has been selected for publishing.
My book has been selected for publishing.
I cry my soul out.

Mr. Doshi must know about this. He will be so proud of me. He will even forgive me. He will know he was right about me the first time. I start typing-
Mr. Doshi,
Please forgive me. I have something huge to tell you that I hope will make up for the disappointment I have caused you. I don't want to tell you over here. Can we meet?
And I hit "SEND".

Epilogue

*Slender strings embark
on a journey
with twists and turns
up and down...
The pattern's perfect
in every shade.*

*The journey is over
but the voyage begins...
The weaving of words
continues...*

www.ingramcontent.com/pod-product-compliance
Lightning Source LLC
LaVergne TN
LVHW041910070526
838199LV00051BA/2573